"He'll be OK," Uncle Grayson assured him. "It's just like when you went in for your arm. They just poke and prod and then tell you what's wrong."

"Will they put his legs in a machine for an x-ray like they did my arm?" he asked and his uncle nodded. "Can I watch?"

"They have to put Rooster to sleep before they do that. It might be a bit scary." His uncle said honestly.

"OK," Wade shook his head emphatically. "I'd rather not."

They walked into a big room and waited for the doctors to finish examining his red horse. When done, there were two veterinarians that sat in the chairs next to them to explain what they needed to do.

Wade couldn't listen. The words were really long and made his head hurt. He looked out the window and watched a lady exercising a horse in the big arena they passed when they arrived.

He heard the word euthanized…he knew that word, Sadie had told him what it meant. It was the one word they didn't want to hear. His heart trembled and his stomach turned. Wade slowly turned his attention back to the adults. All of them were frowning.

COMING SOON

Volume Three of the Series

THE TAGGER HERD:

NIKKI TAGGER

Nikki deals with two mysteries over the holiday vacation. Her adopted mother, Dru, tells her the new client has the same unique name as her birth mother. The two women investigate the stranger; is she or isn't she? If she is, does she know? Rescued horse Arcturus, is losing weight and Nikki needs to find the reason why before the mystery illness becomes life threatening.

RELEASE DATE IS AVAILABLE AT:

www.thetaggerherd.com

FACEBOOK: The Tagger Herd

Cover Artwork: Author Gini Roberge

This novel available from Amazon.com or from the official website of The Tagger Herd Series.

ISBN-13: 978-1499607840

ISBN-10: 1499607849

Printed by CreateSpace
eStore www.CreateSpace.com/The Tagger Herd
Printed by CreateSpace, An Amazon.com Company
CreateSpace, Charleston SC

THE TAGGER HERD SERIES

WADE TAGGER

Gini Roberge

To my son, Tyrel…you light my life.

With heart and soul…love you Sonner

SPECIAL THANKS TO

BEN SMITH, DVM

For Your Input & Output and Editing Expertise

CHAPTER ONE

"I have the most boring dad in the world."

Sitting in the front seat of the truck, his arm wrapped in a bright blue cast from fingers to shoulder, Wade watched his dad talking to the man at the hardware store. His arm was resting comfortably on a pillow on the middle console. As hard as he tried to keep his eyelids up, they fell back down and he was in darkness again.

When they opened, his boring dad was talking on the phone in front of the Kubota tractor store. The collar on his denim jacket was lifted up and the black cowboy hat was pulled down low to protect him from the chilly October day. He hung up the phone when a man came out of the store and handed him a box, "Here you go Scott."

"Thanks Greg…I appreciate this, I didn't want to leave him out here alone," he handed the man a credit card in return and the man went back in the store. His boring dad stood quietly staring down the road until the man returned with his receipt. They shook hands and his dad returned to the truck. Everything went dark again.

When the light returned, they were driving down the road towards the white plumes of smoke coming from the paper mill where his mother worked. Wade loved coming this way because there were trains all over the place. His mom told him they used the trains to move product the mill manufactured.

The train track ran between the road and the security building that led into his mom's work. One of the trains was moving slowly down the track keeping pace with their truck. Its path blocked the entrance to the security gate, so they stopped and waited behind a large semi-truck. As the train cars passed, Wade could see his mother's car in the gap between them. She must have driven from the far side of the manufacturing plant to meet them at the gate.

His head was so heavy it felt like someone had filled it with a bunch of rocks but finally managed to turn his head enough to see his dad. He was watching her car too. Everything went dark again.

Wade could hear his mother's voice but couldn't get his eyes to open to see her. She asked how he was and his dad said he was sleeping a lot then there was silence.

"Jordan," his dad called out. "we need to talk."

Wade managed to get his eyes open long enough to see his mother walking away, carrying papers in her hand, ignoring his dad. See, even his mother thought he was boring.

2

Wade looked up at his dad who was sitting quietly watching her walk away too. Her straight shoulder length black hair was swinging as she walked. She climbed in her car without looking back at them, then turned to drive back to her office building.

Wade sighed…so boring….and his eyes closed again.

When they opened again, they were driving through town, the radio on, his dad humming to the tune…it went dark.

Bells were ringing…the ones that signaled the end of school… his eyes flew open; they were sitting in front of the school. He lifted his tired eyes up to his dad.

"Those pain killers are kicking your butt today," he smiled warmly then reached over to brush Wade's hair away from his eyes. "Are you still hurting?"

"I don't know," it came out as a dry whisper.

He chuckled as he reached down on the floor in front of Wade. "I stopped and got you some Gatorade," a bottle appeared and his dad opened it and lifted it to Wade's mouth. The cool liquid felt good on his lips and down his throat. A few drops ran down his chin. Wade tried to lift his unhurt arm but it was filled with rocks too.

"I'll get it, Buddy," his dad wiped the drops from his chin.

Wade tried to smile, but he wasn't sure it actually happened. He loved his dad calling him Buddy.

"Want another drink?" He was leaning across the truck console so he was close. He smelled good...Wade's eyes closed again.

Somewhere, in the fog in his head, he could hear Sadie talking about Wade's tenth birthday party and Nora was talking about not going to school on Thursday and Friday because of the teacher's conferences.

Wade's eyes opened again and he could see the rodeo grounds...they were headed home. The Homestead was only 5 minutes away from the big arena...everything went dark again.

The truck slowed down and made the turn into The Homestead driveway. His eyes opened to see his dad only drove half way up the drive and stopped. He was pointing his phone at the little herd. The horses had seen the truck and were moving to the fence, some trotting and some walking.

"Can we get out Uncle Scott?" Sadie asked. The door opened before she he answer. She was headed for Little Ghost, it's where she went every night after school. Her parents had to drag her out of the cold barn every night.

"Don't get your school clothes too dirty," he called out to them.

Wade tried to see what his dad was doing with the phone but he had a hard time focusing. When they finally cleared he could see his dad recording the herd as they

4

neared the fence. Wade tried to lift his head to see, "Dad?" he whispered.

"What's up Buddy?" he asked and laid the phone on the seat.

"Can I get out?" his throat was dry making his voice gravelly.

"I don't think that's a good idea right now."

Wade leaned back against the seat. He could feel the tears fill his eyes and tried to make them stop by squeezing his eyelids tight.

He felt a hand on his forehead.

"I'm sorry Buddy," Wade could hear the concern in his voice. His eyes opened to see sad eyes looking back at him. "I know you want to see Rooster and Dollar but you're a bit warm right now," he gently wiped the tear away that had escaped. "I promise we'll come out tonight and see them, but now, you need to get some solid sleep."

"OK…" Wade sighed. His dad would keep the promise, he always did.

The truck started moving and Wade tried to watch the horses as long as he could but everything went dark again. The truck stopped and he heard a door open and close; then the door next to him opened. Wade could feel his dad lean in the truck and pain shot up his arm and shoulder when the casted arm was lifted from the console. Wade groaned loudly and cried out.

"Sorry Buddy, I tried to move it as careful as possible," he was lifted and another groan escaped as the ache began to increase.

"It hurts, Dad." Wade moaned as he leaned into his dad's neck.

"I know Buddy. I'll get you upstairs and get you another pain killer."

"Where's Mavis and Bart?" The cow dogs usually greeted them.

"Up at the ranch with Jessup."

He was carried up to the back deck of the house and he heard the back door open.

"Scott, is he alright?" Wade opened his eyes in time to see Cora's concerned expression.

"Hi Cora," Wade tried to smile at her. She always made him smile and he always felt warm and protected when she was around. He wondered if that's how grandparents made you feel. His eyes started to close again.

"Hi back, young man," she smiled softly and stepped back as he was carried through the door.

"Need pain killers," his dad told her and carried him down the hall toward to the stairs. "They're in the truck."

He felt Matt's big bed engulf him as he was lowered onto it. Matt was at college and the bigger bed was safer for him and the cast. The pillow was adjusted under the casted arm and the pain started to subside. "That's good," Wade whispered.

His eyes opened enough to look up at a very worried expression, "I love you, Dad." he whispered and saw the smile spread across his dad's face.

"Stay awake, just a couple minutes longer, Buddy."

His shoes were removed and since he was wearing sweatpants the blanket was laid over the top of him and tucked in around the sides.

Wade stretched his eyebrows up to keep his eyes open. Cora came in and handed his dad the medicine. After swallowing it, Wade nodded…or tried to…and closed his eyes. A hand touched his forehead again and then nothing.

***

Wade was riding Rooster across the north pasture at the ranch. Dollar, Eli, Scarecrow, Harvey and Arcturus were running next to them. "I wonder where the other horses are," he shouted to Rooster. They galloped across the top of the mountain with trees to the left and pasture to the right. The wind stung at his eyes, but he didn't care, he just reached up and pulled his cowboy hat down lower and tighter. The energy from the horse passed into his legs and up his body so he leaned forward and encouraged Rooster to run faster. Both their hearts were racing.

Wind in his face and the other horses running and jumping over fallen trees and rocks; he was in heaven!

Wade saw his dad's big grey horse Monty run out of the trees next to them. He suddenly felt cold and his heart began beating wildly; this time out of fear instead of excitement. The fear was rising up into his throat, he needed to scream but it wouldn't come out. The large horse's hooves were hitting the ground so hard it made the ground shake and Wade could feel the vibration move through Rooster and into his own stomach.

Monty turned from running with them, to running at them; his eyes seemed to glow red. With each stride Rooster took, Monty took two; he was catching up to them! Steam started coming out of Monty's nose as he ran at them. Wade kicked Rooster harder to make him go faster. He was breathing so hard his lungs hurt and the fear was so intense he thought his heart was going to explode.

Monty was right next to them, he was going to run right into them! Wade needed to keep the grey horse from Rooster. Trying to distract Monty and protect Rooster, Wade screamed and jumped off his red horse.

As he was hurtling through the air, he could hear voices; it sounded like his mom and Matt. Wade looked down and saw the ground getting closer. His whole body tensed to prepare for the imminent impact as he screamed.

"Wade!" It was Matt's voice.

Wade's eyes flew open. There was no pasture or mountains, no Monty, no Rooster. But his heart was racing and he could feel the pain from his arm; it felt like someone was stabbing it.

His mom's scared eyes were looking down at him; Matt was looking just as scared.

Wade didn't say anything but just lay quietly trying to slow down his breathing. A trickle of sweat ran down the side of his face; his mom placed a cool towel on his skin and wiped it away. Her soft touch and gentle smile helped calm his heart.

"That was one heck of a nightmare," she said nervously. Her dark brown, almost black eyes glistened with unshed tears. "Take deep breaths," she demonstrated a deep breath for him. He copied her and they breathed together a couple times…Wade could feel himself gaining control. His lungs didn't hurt anymore.

"I'm OK," he whispered.

"You had us scared there," Matt knelt next to the bed. His cousin's eyes were more green than brown today as Wade smiled up at him. Matt was his hero but he had been gone the last couple weeks at college.

"You're home." Wade told him.

"I came to check on you."

"Are you staying for my birthday?" Wade hoped; his voice was barely a whisper.

Matt grinned, "I wouldn't miss your big double digit birthday, you goof ball." Matt brushed away the hair from Wade's eyes, just like his dad always did. "I have to head back in the morning, but it's only an hour away, so I'll be back in time."

"The party's not until Saturday." Wade reminded him.

"I'll be here Friday." Matt promised.

Behind Matt, his dad appeared at the door with a panicked look; his chest heaved from breathing fast...he must have run up the stairs.

"Hi Dad," Wade smiled. "Matt's gonna be here for my birthday."

His dad's shoulders relaxed, "Jordan...?"

"He was having a bad nightmare and we couldn't get him to wake up," his mom told him. Her voice sounded angry, but his dad just nodded then turned back to Wade with a smile.

"Want to talk about it?" he asked softly.

Wade frowned, he felt the heaviness in his heart come back. He looked down at the cast and didn't say anything...he was too afraid. The tears started building and he had to take deep breaths to make them stop, his chest starting heaving uncontrollably. His lungs hurt from breathing too deep, then the breaths started coming too fast and his head was getting foggy, which scared him.

"Wade, it's OK," he could hear his mom…the tears were running down her cheeks. He was scaring her again too. The guilt made Wade feel even worse and made his tears start flowing and he couldn't stop them. The sob coming up in his throat tasted bad. Before he realized what was happening, he was throwing up then gasping for air.

Matt reached behind and lifted his shoulders so the vomit wouldn't choke him. His dad raced to the other side of the bed and lifted his cast.

"Relax, Wade," Matt whispered to him.

"It's OK, Buddy," his dad spoke softly.

Wade looked into his dad's concerned eyes. His face was just inches away from his own.

"It's OK," his dad tried to reassure him with his eyes.

Wade took a deep breath to try to stop all the little rapid breaths. It made his lungs hurt even more and he started to panic thinking it would never stop. Another breath and his lungs seemed full…he couldn't get any more air in his lungs…he looked up at his parents with terror in his eyes.

His dad grabbed the blankets and threw them off the bed. "Matt, you have a better angle. Pick him up and follow me."

Matt did as he was told and lifted Wade from the bed; his dad helped position the cast over Wade's body. "You got him?"

"Yeah," Matt answered.

Wade looked to his dad then at Matt. He didn't want to go back to the hospital. The panic rose again as they made their way down the hall making Wade gasp again and the air filled his lungs but he started breathing even faster from the fear. His whole body was tingling.

Wade felt the sob coming up again. "I'm going to throw up!" he gasped out between breaths.

"Don't be doing that, kid." Matt started moving faster down the long hallway. "You throw up on me and I'll throw up on you and we'll have a real mess."

Wade looked down through the fog and saw everyone at the base of the steps looking at them. All their faces showed concern…Sadie and Nora were crying. It made him feel worse and the air started coming out of him in large gasps and he dug his face into Matt's neck.

"Backup!" His dad ordered everyone.

"Scott, where are you going?" Wade could hear the panic in his mom's voice.

Wade peeked out from under Matt's chin. His dad didn't answer because he was already out the back door… Matt walking quickly to keep up with him. Wade couldn't stop the panicked breathing…his whole body started to shake.

"No…hospital…" Wade cried. He couldn't tell if it was out loud or not.

His dad ran past the trucks and headed to the barn. Matt was running behind them, Wade bouncing in his arms.

Wade's eyes started to roll back into his head and a blackness was taking over.

The movement stopped.

"Wade!" His dad shouted.

Wade tried hard to open his eyes but couldn't. Someone started lifting his eyelids up for him, so he could see his dad through the haze and then Dollar and Rooster behind him. Their heads were up and ears alert.

The stall door had been opened and a bale of straw placed in front of it. His dad sat down on the end of the bale, straddling it, he reached for Wade. Matt lowered him into his arms and they stretched his legs out over the rest of the bale.

The horse's noses immediately lowered and nuzzled his face. He could feel their breath go down his neck.

"Concentrate on their breathing," his dad whispered in his ear.

Their breath on his skin tickled and he wanted to laugh but his lungs wouldn't let him. He listened to their breathing and tried to match his breaths with theirs. His lungs start to relax and the breathing started to slow down. The fog slowly cleared out of his head.

"There you go. Just look at the horses," his dad's voice made it through the haze.

Wade reached up with his good arm and touched Dollar's face. He loved the smell of horses and the feel of their soft hair. It was thicker now that winter was coming so they seemed fuzzier. He felt something hitting his cast and looked down to see Rooster trying to bite it.

"I think he's trying to free you," Matt said. Wade looked up and smiled. Breathing was easier now; the breaths not as rapid. He had stopped shaking and could see clearly.

"No," Wade whispered to Rooster and gently moved the horse's mouth from the cast. Rooster went for his hand instead to see if there was a treat in it. Wade giggled and leaned back against his dad. He could feel his dad's racing heartbeat against his back; his arms were wrapped tightly around Wade's waist.

"It's OK, Dad, they stopped coming," Wade whispered about the shallow breaths. The arms relaxed.

Rooster turned his attention to Matt and tried nibbling on his hair making Wade grin. Matt turned up his face and blew air up at the horse. Rooster bounced his head up and down then checked Matt's hands for treats.

The strength and warmth from his dad's arms made Wade's body relax. He felt loved and protected; like nothing could hurt him. He looked down at his cast and wiggled the fingers coming out the end, a twinge of fear rose to his heart. If his dad ever found out how he broke his arm, he would lose his dad's love forever.

CHAPTER TWO

It was quiet and comfortable in the barn. Matt had pulled up another bale of straw for a seat and the two men were talking about college classes he liked and didn't like. Matt had thrown hay into the stall to keep the two horses close to the door and Wade. They were grazing quietly. He had fed the other horses too and although Wade couldn't see them, he could hear them eating and moving around. Other than on a tractor with his dad, this was his favorite place on earth.

Uncle Grayson walked into the barn looking even taller than normal from Wade's view on the straw bale. His stomach grumbled when he saw the tray of food his uncle was carrying. He also had a shirt over his shoulder. Wade forgot that he had puked and looked down. There was vomit down the front of his shirt.

"Gross," he whispered.

Matt laughed. "Just be glad you didn't vomit on me going down the hall or we would both be covered in a whole lot more than that."

Uncle Grayson handed Matt the food, then walked into the office. He returned carrying scissors.

Wade chuckled as his uncle cut his shirt off.

"One less shirt in the laundry pile," Uncle Grayson winked.

They carefully maneuvered the clean shirt over his cast and head. He snuggled back into his dad when they were done. "What's for dinner?" Wade asked.

He drank the cup of soup slowly and enjoyed sitting with the men. They were talking about trucks, tractors, and cows; all the good stuff.

Wade glanced over at Rooster who was eating next to Dollar.

It had only been four months since they found the horses in Cora's barn. Rooster's front legs were stuck in the mud and he hadn't been able to move for days. The horse had worn leg wraps for weeks trying to support the ligaments and tendons as they healed but he still walked awkwardly. Nikki and Dr. Mark had worked together on a nutrition plan and the horses were gaining weight.

When Rooster shifted close enough, Matt reached over and patted him on the shoulder then rubbed down his legs to his knees. The red horse stood quietly and took in the attention.

"I took video of him walking today and sent it to Dr. Mark," his dad said. Wade's eyebrows went up; that's what his dad was doing!

"He answer back?" Uncle Grayson asked.

Wade felt his dad move but couldn't tell what the answer was.

"It may be time to take him up to WSU," Uncle Grayson turned to Matt. "Press harder and see if he reacts."

Matt slid his hand down again until he reached the knee. He squeezed lightly then slowly worked his way around the knee. Rooster didn't react so he lifted the hoof and bent the knee as if putting shoes on the horse. Rooster jumped backwards away from him.

"He didn't like that," Wade said, stating the obvious. He looked over at his uncle who had leaned over and was resting his elbows on his knees watching the red horse walk back to Matt. Matt stretched out a hand and petted him, apologizing for hurting him.

"All the horses look a lot better," Wade said. "Rooster's back bone is almost all gone."

"They do look better, Buddy." His dad squeezed him tighter. Wade smiled down into his soup. Even after he scared them tonight and made them worried, his dad still called him Buddy.

"They've all put on a lot of weight," his uncle agreed with him. "Arcturus hasn't gained as much, actually looks like he might be losing. We should talk to Nikki about changing his feed."

Rooster's nose appeared above his soup cup, sniffing it. Wade giggled and tried to get the horse to drink some.

17

His dad stuck his finger in the soup and put it into Rooster's mouth. The horse stuck out his tongue a few times then lifted his head in the air; his upper lip curled up towards the ceiling, showing the pink underneath. He stretched and stretched trying to get rid of the soup.

They all laughed and the sound echoed throughout the barn. Wade turned and could see all the horses come to the stall doors to see what was happening. He loved being in here with all of them. Over the summer, he and the rest of the kids had spent a lot of time with them. They spent more nights sleeping in the barn than they did sleeping in the house.

Rooster finally gave up trying to remove the soup and went back to eating his hay. Wade looked down at the horse's knees. He thought about what his uncle had said about WSU, the hospital for animals in Pullman.

"Dad?" Wade said.

"Yeah?"

"Do you think Rooster will have to have surgery like I did?"

He saw his uncle and Matt look at his dad. There expressions were unreadable.

He felt his dad sigh before he answered, "Yeah, he probably does, son."

Wade turned and looked at the horse, "Will he be OK?"

"I honestly don't know, but before we do any more worrying about him, I'll call tomorrow to see if we can get him up there as soon as possible."

"Can I go too?"

He could see the look of concern on Matt's and his uncle's faces.

"I promise I'll be a grownup. Rooster will be scared going by himself without his friends. He'll need me," he paused, "…like I needed him tonight."

His dad's arms squeezed Wade again and his chin rested on top of his head. "Well, who could argue with that? If it isn't during school hours; I think you'll be missing enough school time with your broken arm."

"I don't think we have school this Thursday and Friday." Wade snuggled into his dad. The soup had warmed him and made him tired.

"We'll see in the morning. I don't know that they will be able to do it that quickly."

"We're headed to Cora's property tomorrow," Uncle Grayson reminded them. "We need to winterize the house."

"She hasn't been there since before her husband died," Matt nodded. "that's going to be tough on her."

Only Aunt Dru had been to the property since they had found the horses. She had driven into the property to check on the place but never left her truck. Wade could

19

barely remember what it looked like, besides the barn, which he remembered as dark and haunting.

He watched Dollar lay down with a plop. The horse groaned; he always did when he lay down. The horse's pelvic bones used to stick out but now there was barely a bone showing. Rooster and Dollar looked so much better; he sighed as his eyes slowly closed.

***

Wade felt the pain in his arm and opened his eyes to see what was wrong…his mind was fuzzy…it took him a minute to realize he was back in Matt's bed. The sky out the window was just starting to lighten. He tried to move but his legs seemed to be stuck. He looked down and saw Nora sleeping at the end of the bed. Wade smiled; it seemed like forever since he'd talked to her.

He tried to move but the arm pain shot through him again. He pushed his foot against his sister to wake her up.

"What?" She gasped frantically as she rolled off the end of the bed, jumped up and looked at him nervously. Her long black hair was loose and looked wild around her head. She was wearing her white pajamas.

He giggled, "You look like a crazy ghost."

She grinned back and lifted her hands over her head and waved them around. They both laughed softly and she climbed back up on the bed.

"Will it hurt if I come up there?"

"It already hurts, so it doesn't matter."

There was just enough room between the cast and the edge of the bed for her to crawl up and lay her head on the other pillow. He and Matt had shared a room. When Matt left for college he told Wade to sleep in his bed when he was away. It was a lot bigger than Wade's bed. He looked over at his bed but Matt wasn't there.

"Where's Matt?"

"He's sleeping downstairs. He didn't want his snoring to wake you up."

They lay quietly for a few minutes before she spoke again.

"You really scared us tonight," she whispered.

"I scared myself."

"What happened?"

"I don't know." He didn't think he could explain it.

"Mom yelled at Dad again."

"For what?" Wade frowned. "It wasn't his fault."

"She said it was because he asked you if you wanted to explain your nightmare."

"We do that all the time…we always talk about our bad dreams to them so the nightmares will go away…it wasn't Dad's fault."

Nora sighed, "I just think she needed to yell at him because he got you to calm down and she just made you cry more."

21

"That's not fair."

"Nope," she turned on her back and then twisted her head so she was facing him. They looked into each other's eyes. "Mom, Aunt Dru, Aunt Leah, and Cora stood outside the barn doors all night holding hands until Dad carried you back in the house. Mom was afraid to go in…she thought it might upset you again."

Wade felt the sadness in his heart again. He hated making them all feel bad. "Do you think I'm the reason they're fighting all the time?"

Nora shook her head with a frown. "No…they were arguing way before your accident. I think it just added to what they argue about."

"Are we supposed to take sides?" he hoped not.

"I don't think so."

"We just wait until they get better?"

"I guess so," she turned back on her side to face him and tucked her hands under her cheek. "Will you tell me how you broke your arm? I promise I won't tell anyone…pinky swear."

Wade turned his head and looked up at the ceiling. He didn't feel the short breathing coming back or the tears. Maybe he should tell her…he needed to tell someone. Then he remembered that the last time he told her a secret she told Sadie. Nora never kept secrets.

He didn't answer but tried to adjust his arm and the pain shot into his shoulder making him grimace.

"Do you want me to get your medicine?" she asked and sat up.

"I don't think they would be happy if you gave me one."

"Do you want me to get Mom or Dad?"

He sighed, "Aunt Dru," he didn't want to make his parents fight again.

***

The next time Wade woke was when Nora climbed out of the bed. Aunt Dru had given him the pain killer and let Nora stay in the room with him. He moved his casted arm a few inches to see if it still hurt. There was a dull ache but not the sharp pain. He used his good arm to adjust it in front of him and tried to sit up. He couldn't get up.

"I feel like a turtle on his back," Wade chuckled.

He was looking around trying to figure out how to get up when his mom appeared at his door. She was smiling warmly.

"Hi, Mom," he smiled back, his voice barely a whisper.

"Feeling better?" She walked into the room, sat next to him and touched his forehead.

"Lots better."

"Well, it looks like your fever broke," she softly ran her finger down his cheek like she had done since he was a baby. He smiled at the touch and her warmth.

"Have the kids left?"

"They're eating breakfast."

"Can I go down too?"

"Of course."

She helped him sit up and slide to the side of the bed then carefully put the sling for the cast over his head and adjusted it tightly around his arm.

"Careful," she put an arm behind his back and one under his cast to help brace him. "You might get a bit dizzy."

Wade stood motionless next to the bed until the dizziness went away. He nodded, "OK."

They walked slowly out the bedroom and down the long hall to the top of the steps and stopped. Looking down long stairwell then to each other, they smiled. "I don't think I can do the steps, Mom."

"Grayson?" She called down the steps.

Wade's head jerked up and he looked at her. Why didn't she call for his dad? Was he gone? Did he scare him away last night? Did he find out what happened and stopped loving him and left? The tightness in his lungs returned and reached his good hand to his chest. He looked down the steps and saw his uncle AND his dad at the bottom. He took a deep breath and the tightness went away.

His dad ran up the stairs while Grayson stayed at the bottom. When he reached the top, he glared at his wife before smiling at Wade. "Good morning, Buddy."

"Hi Dad." Wade grinned. He called him Buddy, so everything was OK.

He was carried down the stairs and into the kitchen where all the kids greeted him excitedly. Matt had already left to go back to college.

Cora gave him a smile and a careful hug then scrunched her face. "You stink, young man."

"He threw up!" Sadie laughed.

"Well, you're going to need a bath before I ride in a truck with you." She ruffled his hair and turned to get his breakfast. Wade's eyebrows shot up in surprise. "Blueberry pancakes...my favorite!" He looked up at Cora with an appreciative grin. "Thank you."

She smiled back. It was the smile that made him feel warm inside. "I was hoping you would have an appetite this morning. Just eat slowly so you don't get sick again."

He nodded and started eating. All the parents and kids came in, greeted him, and slowly left until it was just him, Cora, and his dad sitting at the table.

He took one last bite of pancake and leaned back in the chair. Stomach full, he looked down, he had only eaten half of his normal breakfast but there was no way he could eat more.

He looked up at his dad, "Have you called about Rooster yet?"

His dad laughed, "It's not even 8:00 yet, son."

CHAPTER THREE

Wade sat in the back seat of the truck with his dad on his left side and Cora on the right. His casted arm was resting comfortably on his dad's leg. Uncle Grayson was driving and Aunt Dru was in the shotgun seat in the front. He rested his head back and watched the blue river pass by. The tree's leaves had turned yellow and he liked how the blue and yellow looked together.

His mind went to Rooster. They had sent the video up to the school. The professors and doctors had been reading about the herd's progress on Facebook and the different magazine articles that had been written. Dr. Mark had sent them information about the herd and they were very interested in seeing Rooster. They just had an appointment cancellation for the next day and wanted Rooster brought to them by 10:00 in the morning.

Wade still wasn't going to school so his dad agreed he could go with them to the appointment, if he promised to be an adult. He leaned his head against his dad's shoulder. He had been so eager to go with them earlier, but now, as the time got closer, he felt the nerves in his stomach. He loved Rooster and the thought of him going into surgery just hurt his heart.

"Are you OK?" his dad asked.

Wade looked down and realized he had touched his chest again. He wanted to tell his dad that it was his heart hurting, not his lungs. Instead he leaned his head up and looked at him. He had his brown cowboy hat on and he looked like a cowboy from the movies, "I'm scared for Rooster."

"So am I, son," he sighed. "But if he's in pain, we have to think of what's best for Rooster."

"He doesn't act like he's hurting unless you bend his knee," Wade reminded him.

"We don't really know that. Sometimes you just get used to being in pain," he touched Wade's cast. "Do you still hurt from your arm?"

"Not as much as I did before."

"Is it because it doesn't hurt or because you've gotten used to the pain?"

Wade lifted his arm and realized it did still hurt. "It still aches, but since it doesn't hurt as bad as it was, I don't notice it as much." he admitted.

His dad nodded, "That could be what happened to Rooster. I'm also worried because he doesn't run in the pasture when the other horses start running"

Wade sighed and looked down at his cast, "Will Rooster get worse?"

"It could…as he grows and puts on more weight, it will put a lot of stress on his joints. If he's just putting up with the pain now, then it might become very painful later."

"Do you think there's a chance they can fix him?" He asked hopefully.

"I hope so, Buddy. I really do." He grasped the fingers that were sticking out of the end of the cast. It was the closest he could come to holding his hand.

Everyone had become quiet; listening to their conversation. The truck started to slow down.

Wade looked up and recognized the turn up the dirt road to Cora's house, then turned and looked at her. She was staring down the road, tears rimmed her eyes, and she seemed really pale. He reached over and took her hand and squeezed tightly which made her turn and look at him. She smiled sadly.

"Are you OK?" he asked. She nodded but didn't say anything. "You look kind of sickly." he told her honestly.

She chuckled quietly, "I'm just thinking of the past and all that is back there." she smiled, squeezed his hand and her eyes returned to the road.

Wade looked at his dad; he was looking at her too. His face showed his concern.

They stopped at the gate and Aunt Dru got out and opened it. Wade smiled. It was nice to ride shotgun until you realized you're the one responsible for opening all the gates. This time it wasn't bad but their ranch had four gates to go through before you got to the house.

Aunt Dru left the gate open. They weren't worried about anything getting out or anyone getting in while they were there.

The house was even scarier this time, Wade thought. The sun was hidden behind the clouds so the house looked dark and gloomy. He wondered what it looked like when Cora had lived there. What did the inside of the house look like?

They stopped in front of the house...like last time, they all hesitated before leaving the truck.

Aunt Dru turned in her seat to look at Cora. Her eyes widened in concern, "Are you OK?"

Cora's hand was shaking in his which made him look up at her. She seemed even whiter than she was a few minutes before.

Cora nodded, "I didn't realize it was going to be so hard. It looks so forlorn...and haunted." Wade quietly agreed. Haunted was the word he used the first time they were there.

"Take your time," Uncle Grayson said from the front seat. "We're not in any hurry."

Cora sat quietly in the seat and stared at the house. They all waited for her to reach for the door handle before they did.

As Cora walked to the front door, Wade's dad helped him out of the truck then turned to retrieve the empty boxes out of the back for the items she wanted to take with her.

Wade stood outside and watched the adults disappear into the house. He sighed heavily. As curious as he was to see the inside of her house, he also wanted to go out to the barns. He had to move fast before the adults stopped him. Walking quickly, he passed the house and headed to the upper barn that had held Dollar and Rooster. He turned once to see if he was being watched...no one had seen him yet.

The doors to the barn were closed. He looked down to see if there was any mud blocking the doorway like it was the day they found the horses. No mud but the shovel and hoe were still resting where they left them.

Wade gripped the door with his good arm and pulled hard. He struggled to push it open all the way, having to lean against it and push with his back.

It was just as dark on the inside as he remembered. With one final glance at the house, he stepped into the barn. His mind went back to the first time he had been there. Dollar was the first horse they had seen; in the stall to his left. The horse's big eyes looked at them desperately. Wade walked to the stall and glanced in; the floor was still covered in mud but it was dried and hard. The next stall had been Arcturus' then it was Rufio's.

He was at the back of the barn and looked towards the main doors. It was really gloomy and spooky in there, he couldn't imagine what the horse's felt when they spent weeks alone and starving in such a dark cave.

Across the aisle was Cooper's original stall. Wade looked in…it was the darkest stall of all, which had made it hard to see the black horse when they rescued them. A bucket still lay in the middle of the stall. It looked desolate.

He moved to Little Ghost's stall. The feeder was still lying on the ground and the dark marks of dried blood were on the wall where the horse had cut himself. The wounds were healed but the scars would be pronounced. Sadie didn't care, she loved him anyway. After Angel died, she and Little Ghost had become almost inseparable. Only when she was forced to, did she leave the horse's side. As much as she loved school, she loved the horse more so the beginning of school had been hard on her.

Wade walked to the next stall, Rooster's. He hesitantly walked in and looked at the ground. The holes were still visible where he and Aunt Dru had dug the starving red horse out of the mud. He knelt down, and with his good hand put his fingers in the holes. He closed his eyes and remembered the sad look he and Aunt Dru had shared when they had begun digging at the mud.

"Wade?" Aunt Dru's voice echoed in the barn but he didn't open his eyes. He realized that he was crying again…the sadness of the memory taking over his heart.

His aunt's arm slowly slid around his shoulders and she pulled him into a hug; he leaned his head on her shoulder. They sat quietly for a few minutes remembering those terrible hours.

He opened his eyes and looked up at his aunt. Her eyes were sad but she was smiling, trying to comfort him.

"I want to go into Angel's stall," he whispered. She nodded and helped him stand.

She moved around to his good arm and took his hand then they left the barn and headed down to the lower barn.

"I never did go down to this barn," Wade reminded her. As they came around the corner he stopped and looked at the barn. "It's pretty." he said. It was red with white trim; kind of like the one at home.

He started walking again and she opened the doors. Walking past her, he wandered down the aisle looking into the stalls. They weren't muddy like the other ones.

"This one," Aunt Dru walked into the second stall to the right.

He looked up at his aunt. Her long blond hair was pulled back in a ponytail which was sticking out the back of her ball cap that had the Tagger Enterprise's T3E logo on it. The brown ball cap matched the brown denim jacket she was wearing. "This is a nice barn."

"Yes it is," she agreed.

"I don't know why, but I always thought of them as terrible places." He looked around again. "I don't think Cora would have had a terrible place; she would have nice things."

"You're right. She has nice things."

The comment made him think of the house. "What does the house look like?"

"Let's go up and you can check it out yourself."

"OK."

They walked quietly out the barn and shut the doors behind them. As they walked up to the house, he forgot about the barns; they weren't haunted after all.

Cora's house wasn't very big compared to The Homestead. Wade stood in the large living room and knew Cora was to the left in a bedroom. To the right was another bedroom. In front of him, down a little hallway he could see the bathroom and a kitchen. Just beyond those was a utility room. That was it. He figured they didn't need much more for only two people.

He looked at the pictures on the tables. One of Cora and her husband caught his attention. It was the first time he had seen Wes. He wasn't much taller than Cora and was wearing a grey cowboy hat. Wade looked closer. Their arms were around each other and they looked really happy.

"We were at my sister's 50th birthday party in that picture," Cora's voice came from behind him.

"You look happy."

"We always were," she smiled.

She took the picture he was looking at and put it in the box she was packing. He helped her gather the rest of the pictures and put them in the box.

Wade continued to look around. He didn't see anyone else, "Where is everyone?"

"They turned all the water off and prepared the house for winter, so I sent them out to the tack room to get everything. No sense it being stolen or ruined up here. We can put it to use at The Homestead or the ranch."

She continued to pack so he wandered down the hallway to the kitchen. There was a single plate, fork and coffee mug in the sink. A heavy layer of dust covered them. Wade frowned at them. They were from Wes' last meal... a sadness came over him which made him look down the hall to Cora. If he felt that sad...how bad was it for her?

Wade looked around the kitchen...everything was covered with dust but it was orderly and there were pretty plates decorated with birds on the wall. They were nice and he was sure that she wanted them so he carefully took them from the wall and placed them on the table.

Another glance at the fork, plate, and mug in the sink
…he didn't want her to see such a sad sight, so with a
little difficulty he washed and dried and put them away.

He heard his dad talking to Cora in the living room.
Wade turned and went to the bedrooms. They were nice
too.

"Cora?" He called as he walked down the hallway to
find a box for the bird plates. He turned the corner and
saw her leaning against the wall, holding her stomach.
"Cora! Are you OK?" He hurried to her, took her arm and
walked her to the chair.

"I'm fine, hon." she smiled up at him.

"No you're not." he started to walk past her to get his
dad.

"No you don't." she grabbed his arm. She might be
sick but she still had a pretty strong grip.

"I need to go get Dad, you're sick." he argued.

"Just a little emotional," she assured him. Wade
frowned…he knew it was more than that.

"I have something for you," she changed the subject.

"I don't want anything but Dad to help you."

She chuckled. "Wade, I'm fine," she leaned back
around the chair. "It's an early birthday gift." she
explained and pulled out a lariat.

Wade gasped. It was a big one, like his dad and
uncles.

"This was my husbands," she handed it to him.

He slowly raised his good arm and took the rope.

"I gave this to him a few years ago for his birthday."

Wade didn't know what to say. He just looked at the lariat in amazement. It was coiled perfectly. He rubbed his thumb over the ridges of the rope and bounced it in his hand to feel the weight.

"On the ride back to the house, I'll tell you about some of Wes' best roping moments."

"I wish I could have met him," Wade smiled at her.

"He would have like you. He had a lot of respect for kids that were hard workers like you, your sister, and cousins."

"How come you didn't have kids?"

"Wes couldn't have them and we never really decided to adopt…then it just got too late in life. My sister had five kids and they had kids…she has twelve grandchildren. We go visit them during the summer and at Christmas. I like Christmas with kids around."

"Does it bother you to talk about him?"

"It did at first, but now I like to talk about him."

"Will you tell me stories about him? I'd like to know."

She smiled gently at him, it was the smile that made him feel warm inside.

"I'd love to," she looked around the room. "We have a couple photo albums around here somewhere."

"Over here," Wade said and walked to the bookshelf. He lifted the books and put them in one of the boxes.

"Thanks, can you put the other books in there too?"

Wade nodded and placed all the books in the box. "There's some bird plates in the kitchen…I just need a box."

"Oh, good…I love those plates. Wes gave one to me each year on Valentine's Day."

She went to stand up and fell back in the chair.

Wade didn't wait for her to stop him this time…he ran out the door yelling for his dad.

He turned the corner of the house towards the barn where they were loading the tack into the truck. His dad had started running up to the house. His aunt and uncle right behind him.

They began to slow down when they saw Wade, so he waved at them to move faster. "It's Cora!" He yelled. His dad and uncle ran passed him; his aunt turned around and ran to the truck.

Wade barely made it to the door when he heard the truck start and the engine grow louder as Aunt Dru was racing to the house.

Both men were kneeling next to Cora when Wade made it back into the house. She was reassuring them that she was fine, but had just lost her balance when she tried to get up. Wade had run out the door before she could stop him. The men looked at each other; by the looks on their faces, they didn't believe her either.

The lariat was lying in the middle of the floor…he didn't realize he had dropped it. He quickly picked it up and sat in the corner chair to stay out of the way as they loaded the boxes Cora had packed. He told Aunt Dru about the bird plates and she carefully packed them.

Wade watched Cora who had leaned back in the chair and closed her eyes. They weren't letting her get out of the chair. Her hair had grown a lot since they first met her; it was now down to her shoulders. She looked younger than the 68 she said she was. Before today she always seemed healthy; she did her yoga exercise every morning.

He stood as they started turning off lights. Uncle Grayson helped Cora out of the chair but she insisted on walking without help.

As they rode back to The Homestead, Wade ran his fingertips over the ridges of the rope following the coiled length of it. He was worried about Cora who was asleep next to him.

She was still sleeping when they parked in front of the doctor's office. Aunt Dru had quietly called them and made an appointment for Cora.

When his dad opened the door, her eye's flickered open and her body stiffened. She was instantly upset.

"I'm not going in there!" she glared.

"You don't have a choice about that," he reached out to her. "Your only choice is if I'm carrying you in or are you walking in?"

CHAPTER FOUR

Wade held the back door open while his dad helped Cora walk into the kitchen of The Homestead. She smiled and thanked him politely.

Behind Cora, Aunt Dru walked up the steps of the patio.

"She'll be fine," Aunt Dru assured him. "The doctor gave her some medicine that will help her out."

Wade nodded. He turned and saw his uncle start to unload the tack from the truck into the barn.

"Can I go help Uncle Grayson?" he asked.

"Sure."

The screen door slammed behind him and he carefully stepped down the patio steps. He started running across the driveway to the truck; his new lariat bouncing on his shoulder.

Uncle Grayson came out of the barn, "Stop running." he ordered. "The last thing we need is for you to fall and re-break that arm."

Wade slowed down to a walk, "Would it break again with the cast on?"

His uncle grinned, "You want to find out?"

Wade grinned back, "No."

He handed Wade a saddle pad to take into the barn. The barn was too quiet. All the horses were out in the pasture and Mavis and Bart were at the ranch. Thinking of the dogs up at the ranch was depressing. It was because the family left so fast the night he broke his arm, that they were left at the ranch and not down here with all the kids.

Wade helped unload the truck the best he could. With each trip in the barn he felt his energy waning and he began to drag his feet. When they were done with the tack going in the barn, the truck was backed up to the deck so they could unload Cora's boxes.

Wade held the door open as his uncle carried the boxes into the house and back to Cora's room. He leaned his head back on the door frame as he waited for him to return. The lariat was in his hand; the end resting on the floor. Wade meant to close his eyes for just a second, but it must have been longer. His head jerked down and to keep from falling, he threw it backwards and banged it into the door. "Dang," He mumbled and then he heard the laughing. He opened his eyes to see his dad, aunt, and uncle standing in the kitchen watching him. He gave them a tired smile.

"Come on," his dad reached out to take his hand. "You may be 'almost ten' but I think you need a nap."

Wade took a couple steps and realized just how tired he really was, "Dad?"

He stopped and looked down at him.

"I've gotten used to you carrying me," he smiled. "And I'm really, really tired."

The adults laughed at him again as his dad leaned down and picked him up.

"Can I just sleep on the couch and not in bed?" Wade leaned his head on his dad's shoulder.

"Sounds like a good idea Buddy." He leaned his chin on top of Wade's head so he missed the smile that spread across his sons face when he called him Buddy.

***

Wade woke and heard the adults talking at the small table in the kitchen. He leaned forward to see if Cora was with them. She wasn't. He leaned back and looked at the clock. It was only one o'clock which meant the kids wouldn't be home for over an hour. He sat up so the sleepiness would leave his head. The lariat was on the floor so he picked it up and set it in his lap and with the tip of his finger traced the coiled rope.

Cora must still be napping. She really didn't look good when she came out of the doctor's office. Although she wasn't in there very long, she seemed worse, not better. He leaned his head on the back of the couch. What if the same happened to Rooster? What if he went into the clinic and came out worse? What if he didn't come out? What if Cora didn't get better?

He shook his head really hard to get the bad thoughts out.

All the bedrooms were upstairs, except for Cora's, and the guest bedroom which Nikki used when she came home from college. He looked down the hall to see if Cora's bedroom door was closed but couldn't see that far down the hall. He wanted to talk to her but he was nervous. What if she got worse while he was sleeping?

He felt the depression in his heart. How could he lose both Cora and Rooster?

The dust covered dishes from Wes' last meal flashed in his mind...how sad was that image!

Wade listened to The Trio for a few minutes. He couldn't hear what they were saying, just that they were talking.

How did they make it through the accident that killed their parents and grandparents? The sadness was heavy just THINKING about losing Rooster and Cora. Wade couldn't imagine losing his parents. How did they do it?

He stood up slowly in case the dizziness returned. It didn't, so, lifting his rope over the shoulder with the cast, Wade walked slowly towards the kitchen. With his boots off, he didn't make a sound and their talking continued. They were at the table with their cattle books scattered in front of them. Aunt Dru was writing something in one of the books.

He leaned on the door-jam and watched them for a minute before he blurted out. "How did you do it?"

They looked at him in surprise. "Do what?" His dad asked.

"How did you handle the sadness of the accident?" He didn't have to say what accident; they knew.

They didn't answer; they froze in place. Wade thought they looked like they were playing a game of statue. His aunt stared at him in shock, pencil frozen in place, tears sprung to her eyes. His uncle had been lifting his glass to take a drink and it was frozen in mid-air. His dad had been reaching for one of the work books and his hand froze in place over it. They just stared at him.

"Never mind," Wade sighed and turned away from them and headed down the hallway. He stopped half way and leaned against the wall; depression making it too hard to walk. If they weren't handling the loss, eighteen years later, then how would he be able to handle losing Rooster and Cora?

"Well, we handled that well." he heard Aunt Dru say. They must have thought he had left.

"I don't think that's called handling it at all." his dad answered.

"Where do you think that came from?" Uncle Grayson asked.

"Rooster," his dad answered.

"Probably Cora this morning too," Aunt Dru added.

They were quiet so long he almost left.

"I lost count on how many times people told me I was handling 'it' well or asked me how I was handling 'it', after the accident," His uncle said and sighed heavily.

"How can anyone handle 'it'?" Aunt Dru asked. "One foot in front of the other, one breath after the other, one day goes by, then the next."

"I think it was Matt and Nikki," His uncle said.

"Yeah," she agreed. "Focusing on those two kept me sane."

Wade heard a chair move and footsteps. He waited for them to come into the hall. Instead he heard someone moving away from him then walking back to the table. The chair moved again as they must have sat back down.

"Are you going to talk to Wade?" Aunt Dru asked.

"I honestly don't know what to say," his dad admitted. "Until you go through something like that, you don't know how to handle it."

"Well," Wade heard his dad say. "Next time…you two need to handle questions like that better."

Wade could tell he was joking.

"Us?" His aunt and uncle asked in unison.

"Yeah," his dad chuckled. "I'm the baby brother. I shouldn't have to answer the tough questions."

"It was your son that asked!" Aunt Dru laughed.

"It was your nephew," his dad responded with a chuckle.

A chair moved across the floor making Wade hurry down the hall towards Cora's room. Her door was open, so he peeked around the corner to see if she was awake.

Cora's bedroom wasn't as big as the adult rooms upstairs, they were like mini apartments, but it was big enough to have her bed and a small sitting area next to the big window. There was also a large private bathroom. She was sitting in one of the chairs staring out the window. She saw him and waved him in.

"Are you feeling better?" he asked and walked to the chair across from her. He glanced out the window and saw the herd of horses.

"I am," she smiled. "I was just sitting here watching those beautiful horses," she sighed. "It's so relaxing just watching them wander the pasture grazing."

He pulled his legs up into the chair and settled his lariat on top of them.

"Thank you for the lariat."

"You're welcome. I'm impressed you call it a lariat and not a rope."

"Dad taught me."

"You have a good dad."

Wade nodded, "Are you going to be OK?"

"I am," she shifted in her chair so she faced him. "The doctor gave me some medicine to help. I had a bad reaction to the new vitamins I started taking, so it's not contagious."

"You scared me," he said honestly.

"And you've scared me the last few days," she countered.

"You looked sad when I came in. I'm feeling really sad about you and Rooster."

"I'll be fine…going back to the house…the memories are tough sometimes…and I'm concerned about Rooster too."

"How do you handle the sadness?"

"Patience," she said softly. "Knowing that it will start to ease and something good will come along and make you forget the sadness for a while. Each time that happens, it eases the loss a little more." She glanced out the window. "Watching the horses...they remind me of how much Wes loved me, and that helps to ease the pain," she looked back at him. "Wes' gift ultimately led me to a whole new family and I adore each and every one of the Tagger herds; horse and human. Being around you and the rest of the kids just fills me with energy."

"I like having you here," he smiled at her. Just talking to her made him feel better.

"I like the ranch too," she commented.

Wade sighed and leaned back against the chair and glanced around. He didn't want to talk about the ranch, so he looked for something to change the subject. He saw her TV and DVD movies lying next to it. "You were watching a movie?"

"Just finished one of my favorites," she smiled at him. "A John Wayne movie, of course."

He sat back up, "Which one?"

"*The Quiet Man.*"

"That's a good one…Mom's favorite," he nodded. "Have you seen *The Cowboys*? It's my favorite. I'd love to be one of the boys."

She chuckled, "I have the DVD over there in that box if you'd like to watch it. It was one of Wes's favorites too."

Wade glanced down at his cast and wiggled his fingers at the end of it. "Nah, what other ones do you have?"

"You don't want to watch *The Cowboys*?" She asked in surprise.

"Does that one of that bad word in it?"

"No, we bought the edited one. Neither Wes nor I liked that word."

"Me either,"

"Do you want to watch it?"

He just shook his head.

"Alright," she gave him a concerned smile. "Go ahead and pick one out. Wes had all kinds of westerns. I love them all."

Wade stood and went to the box next to the TV. He picked up the DVD box that held *The Cowboys* and looked at the cover…John Wayne…each of the kids…he set it aside. He was going through the rest of the movies when his dad came to the door.

He talked to Cora for a few minutes before turning his attention to Wade. "Did you want to talk?"

Wade didn't want to talk about sadness anymore so he just shook his head, "No, it's OK Dad. Cora and I are just gonna watch a movie and rest."

His dad nodded and reached to pick up *The Cowboys* DVD. "Watching this again?" He smiled, but the smile left when Wade shook his head.

"Nah," he looked back into the box so he didn't have to see his dad's reaction and ignored the uneasy feeling in his stomach. "I'm looking for something different."

It was quiet for a few minutes; Wade kept going through the movies. He wasn't really seeing them; he was just trying not to turn around to his dad.

"So what other choices do you have?" He finally asked. Wade picked up the next one in line and without looking at it handed it to him.

"No, I don't think so." He chuckled. Wade looked and saw it was a movie with Clint Eastwood, *The Unforgiven*. It was R rated. He quickly looked in the box and saw another favorite movie and handed it to his dad.

"*Silverado*," he nodded. "That's more like it."

"It's a fun one, so it will lift our spirits," Cora smiled.

His dad put his hand on top of Wade's head and when he didn't look up, he moved his hand down and put a finger under Wade's chin and lifted it up. Wade looked up at him and tried to smile. He didn't think it worked too well because his dad's expression was concerned.

"We're going out back to go through Cora's tack," Dropping his hand from Wade's chin he continued. "you let me know if either of you need anything."

"We will." Cora assured him.

Wade didn't say anything…he was afraid his voice would show his nervousness. He nodded and concentrated on putting the movie in the player.

Wade could see Cora in the mirror nodding at his dad. Her expression showed her concern too.

Wade crawled back in the chair next to Cora. Part way through the movie Sadie, Grace, and Nora arrived home and jumped on the bed to quietly watch it with them.

Wade must have fallen asleep, because he could feel himself being lifted. Then there was the motion of climbing the steps, a feeling of the pillows on Matt's bed surrounding him.

"I tried to get him to talk about the ranch, but he just changed the subject," he heard Cora say.

"Did he say why he didn't want to watch *The Cowboys*?" His dad was talking. Wade kept his eyes closed so he didn't have to answer their questions.

"No," Cora answered. "he just picked it up, looked at it for a minute then set it down again."

"That doesn't make any sense," his dad said. "he loves that movie…there's been times he would watch it two or three times in a row…on the same day."

Their voices began to drift as they walked down the hall.

Wade opened his eyes and stared at the ceiling wondering if he was ever going to be able to watch that movie again.

CHAPTER FIVE

Wade woke early and wiggled himself down into the blankets, they were warm and soft and he didn't want to get up yet. He opened an eye and glanced at the other bed; it was empty. Reilly was at home and Matt was in college. He always wondered what it would be like to have his own room and now that he had it, he wasn't sure he really liked it.

He heard footsteps in the hallway and harsh whispers. It had to be Sadie and Nora, they argued all the time. He wasn't sure how Grace could stand to share a room with them. The three girls shared one large room with big rugs on the floor to designate which part of the room belonged to which girl. There were fancy room separators blocking the girls sections from each other.

Wade and Matt didn't need a separator; they got along really well for their eight year age difference. Wade's side of the room was covered in tractors; toys, replicas, and posters. There were pictures lined up on a long shelf of Wade at various ages riding with his dad in the Tagger Enterprises tractors. Some of his best days, in his whole ten years, were spent farming with his dad.

Matt liked them too but his side was more 'mature' with family snapshots, pictures taken at the ranch, and a few baseball trophies he had won with the teams he played with in school and over the summer. There was one large picture of deer at the ranch. So both boys liked each other's side of the room and got along well.

The girl's whispers faded as they made their way down the hall and staircase.

Wade debated whether to stay in bed or go referee the two again. He closed his eyes and tested whether he was going to be able to go back to sleep…his mind went to Rooster and the impending trip to WSU. Lifting the covers off him with his good arm he decided to get up, he wouldn't be able to go back to sleep anyway. He needed his mind busy until they were ready to go. Might as well let the two arguing girls do that for him.

He positioned the cast over his stomach and rolled onto his good side. Using his legs to move himself to the side of the bed, he pushed with his good arm to sit up. The dizziness just lasted a few seconds then he put the sling over his head and cradled his arm in it. He headed out the door and to the barn where he knew the girls would be.

They were still arguing when he walked in, just louder.

"I just asked a dang question, Sadie." Nora grumbled.

"I don't know why you did," Sadie answered tersely.

"What are you two arguing about this time?" Wade asked as he held out his coat for one of them to help him put it on.

They both moved forward and helped. Neither one answered his question.

"Is it that stupid that neither of you want to tell me?" Wade smirked.

Nora shrugged and moved into the stall with Arcturus and Scarecrow. Sadie stood on the outside and glared in at Nora.

The girls looked as different to each other as the two horses did. Sadie was tall for her age, her mom at 5' 10" and her dad stood 6' 3". She also took after their light complexion, blonde hair and blue eyes. Nora was shorter even though she would be turning 12 in November; a week after Sadie turned 10. Nora and Wade both took after their mother's Native American coloring along with dark brown eyes and black hair. Since their mom was barely 5 foot tall, Nora didn't have a chance to catch Sadie in height. He desperately hoped he would.

The only thing the two girls had in common was their long hair. Sadie's hair was to her waist, Nora's only half way down her back. Both girls had their hair loose this morning with just a headband holding it back.

Scarecrow was a golden palomino with white mane and tail. Arcturus was totally black except the star on his forehead. After putting the weight back on, Scarecrow was turning out stockier than Arcturus' more long and elegant conformation.

Little Ghost, Sadie's grey horse, was in the next stall. Sadie stopped glaring at Nora and entered his stall.

Dollar and Rooster were on the opposite side of the aisle from Little Ghost so Wade turned to them as Nora walked her two horses out of the barn and headed for the pasture. She would go directly to the house to get ready for school instead of coming back to the barn after letting them go.

Jack had dropped Reilly off to catch the bus with Grace, and the two teenagers had already put their horses in the pasture, along with Trooper and Harvey.

"Want me to halter Dollar for you?" Sadie asked.

"Nah, he can stay in here and keep Rooster company until we leave."

"I'll get some hay for them," Sadie headed to the bale at the barn door.

Wade opened the door to the stall when she returned. Both horses made it difficult for her to get to the feeder but Sadie just laughed at them.

"What were you arguing about this time?" Wade asked as she walked out of the stall and headed back to Little Ghost.

A shoulder shrugged as she reached for the horse's halter that hung on a hook just outside the stall. "She asked me if she should thin down Scarecrow's mane to keep it shorter or just let it grow."

"What did you say?"

"That she needed to make up her own mind…it wouldn't matter what I said…she would just do the opposite."

Wade nodded, that part was probably true. "Why didn't you tell her the opposite?"

Sadie shrugged as they walked along with the grey horse and out of the barn.

"Scarecrow is hers…"

"So?"

"I wouldn't let anyone else make that decision about Little Ghost."

"And she wouldn't for Arcturus," Wade opened the gate to the pasture for her to walk through. "So why would she about Scarecrow?"

"I don't know," Sadie turned back to the barn.

Aunt Leah was standing on the back deck of the house, "Sadie hurry up, you need to eat and leave in the next 5 minutes."

"Ok, Mom." Sadie answered.

"Why do we go through this every morning?" Aunt Leah asked but, not expecting an answer, walked back into the house.

Wade and Sadie grinned at each other and walked toward the back of the house.

He glanced at his cousin and wondered if he should talk to her about his arm. She always kept secrets and they had a lot between the two of them.

"Sadie?"

"What?"

Wade wiggled his fingers at the end of the cast, "How come you never asked me how I broke my arm?"

Sadie stopped at the bottom of the steps and looked at him; her brows wrinkled together showing her seriousness. "We share everything."

He nodded.

"Well, I figured, if you wanted to tell me, you already would have."

Wade looked into her blue eyes and sighed, "It's just that…"

"It's OK, Wade," her eyes softened. "You have your reasons."

Wade looked down at his cast and wiggled his fingers again. He nodded.

"Then, when you're ready, I'll be here for you to talk to," she smiled at him to let him know she wasn't upset.

Her mother opened the door, "Get in here."

Sadie grinned again and headed up the stairs.

Wade sat on the bottom step and rested the cast on his lap. He stared out at the barn, thinking of Sadie and Nora…wondering why they couldn't go a day without arguing. The back door opened and closed.

His mother sat down next to him and took his right hand and squeezed.

"I wish I was going with you today."

"It's OK, Mom," Wade smiled to reassure her.

"Work is just…there's a deadline…" she exhaled. "I don't know…"

Wade squeezed her hand tightly, "Dr. Mark said it was just like a checkup today, he'll be home tonight."

"But I should be there with you."

Wade turned and looked into her tear filled eyes, "I love you Mom, and I know you love Rooster, too."

She nodded and exhaled loudly.

"It's Ok," he told her again.

"If he has to have surgery, I don't care what's going on at work…I'll be there for you."

The back door opened. Nora, Sadie, and Aunt Leah walked out.

"Jordan, they missed the bus again," Aunt Leah told them.

"I'll drop them off on the way to work again," his mom said. She squeezed his hand then leaned over and kissed the top of his head. "I'll be thinking of you and Rooster."

As Sadie passed by him, she looked down and had a guilty twinkle in her eye. Wade grinned and watched them leave. It was their secret. When they didn't feel like riding the bus…they spent too much time in the barn in the morning so a parent would take them in.

He looked down at his cast and wiggled his fingers…secrets…so many secrets…but his was the biggest of all. He wasn't going to tell Sadie, he didn't want to burden her with having to keep it. The consequences of the truth were too great.

CHAPTER SIX

Wade stood behind the trailer and watched his dad and Uncle Grayson try to load Rooster into it. They were headed to WSU for Rooster's appointment, but Rooster was not going into the horse trailer. No matter what they tried, the horse wouldn't go in.

"Wade!" His dad called out.

"Yeah?"

"Let's see if he'll go in if you're in there."

"OK," he said and his uncle braced him as Wade stepped into the trailer.

Wade looked into the horse trailer. It wasn't the stock trailer that was more open and airy. It was the one that had closed windows to protect the horses. He walked inside and looked around.

"Wade?" He heard his dad's voice. "What are you doing?"

Wade walked back to the narrow opening which was only half the width of the trailer due to the tack room on the other side.

"Checking it out to see why Rooster doesn't like it." Wade answered.

His dad looked up at him, hands on hips. "And what did you find out?"

He smiled at his dad, who wasn't wearing a hat yet but still looked like a western movie star. He was smiling up at his son.

"Come in and I'll show you," Wade said and walked back in. He figured it would be easier to show them. Only his dad stepped in.

"You too, Uncle Grayson!" Wade called out and his Uncle stepped into the trailer.

Wade looked out and saw his aunt walking towards them.

"What are you guys doing?" she asked. "It's supposed to be the horse in the trailer, not you guys."

Wade chuckled, "Can you come in?"

She stepped into the trailer so he had all of the Tagger Trio standing next to him. He looked up at all three of them. "Do you see it?" He asked his aunt.

She looked around and finally nodded.

"What?" His dad and Uncle Grayson asked in unison.

"It looks dark and scary like the stalls at Cora's property." Wade told them. It reminded Wade of the day before when he revisited the barn and looked from the back of the barn to the front…if he was Rooster, he wouldn't want to go in either.

They both looked around and slowly nodded.

"Smart young man," his uncle said and walked out of the trailer, followed by his dad and Aunt Dru. She turned and helped Wade step out of the trailer.

His uncle was already climbing in the truck to move the trailer and unhook it. He hooked up the stock trailer to the truck instead. Once done, Rooster went into the open airy stock trailer without a problem.

During the drive the adults were worked hard on keeping the conversations going, trying to keep Wade from thinking about the appointment. Wade just sighed...at least they were trying.

They made it to the top of the Lewiston hill grade and pulled over to check on Rooster. The highway out of the valley was a long gradual climb, but you had to do it to get to Pullman and the University. His dad opened the back of the horse trailer and braced Wade as he climbed in to check on his horse. Wade used his good arm and patted the horse's nose and made sure he was alright.

"He's OK Dad."

They made it the rest of the way to the University without having to stop.

When Uncle Grayson pulled up next to a large brick building, Aunt Dru slid out of the truck and walked through large glass doors. They waited quietly until she finally came out and told them the directions to take Rooster. They drove around to the back of a large building with a lot of white framed entrances in it. Wade could see a horse arena that looked like a race track. On the outside; the place looked nice.

Wade stood at the foot of the horse trailer waiting for his dad to walk Rooster out.

The horse groaned when he stepped down off the back of the trailer. Wade cringed inside, wondering how painful it was for him.

He reached out for the lead rope but his dad shook his head.

"Sorry Buddy, this is a strange area for him and lots of things that could spook him. I don't want him accidently hitting your cast."

Wade nodded with a dejected sigh and followed behind the group of adults as they walked into the building, his lariat swinging over his shoulder.

There was a really wide hallway they walked down and toward other horses that were already there. They looked like they were in cages not stalls which made Wade start to get nervous. In different rooms he saw big machines, he heard the doctors say they were used for testing. That made his heart really race.

There were so many long words being tossed around that they all started to sound like a foreign language. He pushed his lariat up high on the shoulder that had the cast and looked around for the first hand that belonged to a family member. He reached out and grabbed ahold and squeezed. His uncle looked down supportively and squeezed back.

They walked by a room that had large pipe stalls like Dr. Mark had at his clinic.

Then they walked by a hole in the ground that looked like a miniature swimming pool. The lady in a white jacket said it was for horses. His eye's widened. She smiled and said it was for the horses to rehabilitate from injuries.

"Will Rooster go in there?"

She nodded, "More than likely; but it will depend on the type of surgery he has and how he needs to exercise to recover."

The lady followed them around and explained different scary thing to him. By the time she was done, he wasn't as nervous anymore; but he kept ahold of his uncle's hand...just in case.

A man in a white jacket took Rooster away...Wade didn't even get a chance to say goodbye to him. He took a deep breath and let it out slowly to keep himself calm.

"He'll be OK," Uncle Grayson said. "It's just like when you went in for your arm. They just poke and prod and then tell you what's wrong."

"Will they put his legs in a machine for an x-ray like they did my arm?" He asked and his uncle nodded.

"Can I watch?"

"They have to put Rooster to sleep before they do that. It might be a bit scary." His uncle said honestly.

"OK," Wade shook his head emphatically. "I'd rather not."

They walked into a big room and waited for the doctors to finish examining his red horse. When done, there were two veterinarians that sat in the chairs next to them to explain what they needed to do.

Wade couldn't listen. The words were really long and made his head hurt. He looked out the window and watched a lady exercising a horse in the big arena they passed when they arrived.

He heard the word euthanized...he knew that word, Sadie had told him what it meant. It was the one word they didn't want to hear. His heart trembled and his stomach turned. Wade slowly turned his attention back to the adults. All of them were frowning.

"You're not going to kill him are you?" Wade asked calmly, trying to sound like an adult. They all turned and looked at him. His uncle squeezed his hand tightly.

"Wade," his dad answered with soft, concerned eyes. "You wanted us to be honest with you?"

Wade nodded.

His dad continued, "If there isn't a way to get Rooster out of pain, it may have to happen. It would be best for Rooster."

Wade just stared at him for a minute then turned his eyes back to the lady exercising the horse in the arena. Why did he keep asking them to be honest with him?

They should lie to him and tell him everything is fine. He felt like he was in a bad dream. A different kind of nightmare than the one he had about Monty.

The horse in the arena with the lady changed from a walk to a trot as he went in circles. Then he moved to a gallop. He looked like he was in good shape. Wade wondered if that would be Rooster someday. Maybe he would come up here and watch the lady exercising Rooster, not euthanizing him.

He concentrated on the horse moving and the feel of his Uncle's hand holding his own. It always surprised him when just holding hands made him feel better. It made him feel like he wasn't alone. Wade glanced up at his uncle and wondered if it felt the same way to him.

Uncle Grayson noticed him looking up at him and smiled down, his blue eyes looking concerned. "You OK?" he whispered.

Wade shrugged his shoulders, "I don't know." He looked at the other adults who were still discussing Rooster's legs.

"Do you understand what they're saying?"

Wade shook his head. "Just the part about putting him to sleep if he's in pain," he sighed. "I guess that's the important part." He felt like crying, but told himself to be strong for Rooster. "When can we take Rooster home?"

His uncle leaned down a little more so he didn't disturb the other adults.

"He should be awake enough in about a half hour so we can take him home. Then we'll decide on a surgery date for him to come back."

Wade nodded. His dad turned to him and glanced between him and Uncle Grayson. His uncle nodded to let him know everything was OK.

The other adults stood so Wade and his uncle did too.

It was a very quiet ride home. The Trio didn't want to talk about Rooster with Wade there but he wanted all the kids to know what happened today.

He was in the back seat with his dad so he looked up and asked; "Can we have a family meeting?"

"About?"

"I think it would be better to tell everyone about Rooster at the same time. So it doesn't have to be said over and over again."

His dad nodded, "I think that's a great idea."

They arrived in Lewiston in time to swing by the junior high school and give Grace and Reilly a ride home. They were both excited about not having to ride the bus but bummed they wouldn't be told about Rooster until the family meeting.

Rooster groaned and Wade cringed again as the horse stepped out of the trailer. Wade led him to the south pasture to join the rest of the herd with Dollar and

Buttercup trotting to the fence to greet them. Grace had followed Wade to open the gate.

"Thanks," he told his cousin as they turned from the gate. Wade made his way to the front steps and sat to watch the herd graze…or try to since the grass had gone dormant. They put the horses in the pasture for exercise.

Grace sat on the step next to him.

"I like just sitting here watching them." Grace said softly.

"Me too."

"You OK?" She asked without looking at him.

"I don't know."

"Want to talk about it?"

"What?"

"Whatever…I'm always here for you to talk to."

"I know."

"Well?"

Wade sighed, "I'm worried about Mom and Dad…Rooster…and Cora…and then there's all that homework Sadie is going to be bringing me from school today."

"Who ever said that being ten was easy?" Grace grinned at him which helped raise his mood. She had the best smile and her laugh could brighten the darkest of days.

"I'm still nine for a couple days," Wade reminded her. "Hopefully ten will be easier than nine."

Grace nodded, "Then there is the arm…"

"Yep," Wade wiggled his fingers at the end of the cast. "Then there's that…"

He trusted her…but he wouldn't tell her either…for the same reason he wouldn't say anything to Sadie.

They sat quietly and watched the horses until Sadie and Nora arrived…then their mom's and Jack arrived from work and the family meeting was called.

Everyone gathered at the table and chairs on the back deck. The temperature had warmed for the day, so they took advantage of one of the last times to gather there before winter weather started.

Wade looked around at all the kids and adults gathered to hear about Rooster. Reilly was sitting next to him. Jack and Cora were sitting next to Aunt Dru. He looked down at the lariat in his lap when his dad started talking. He was listening intently this time because he knew his dad wouldn't use all the long words.

Rooster didn't just have knee problems. His hocks, the ankle for a horse, were also damaged and causing the issues.

There was the possibility that surgery could be attempted that would ease the pain and possibly repair it all together so he could have a normal life. The other kids were excited and hopeful until he raised his hand to quiet them down. That was never good.

The doctors believed that if they did surgery, they would find that he was either too injured to save and would be in pain the rest of his life, or they could ease the pain but not eliminate it. Either way, he wouldn't be able to have a normal life.

Everyone was quiet.

His dad spoke directly to the kids. "The most important thing to do is what is best for Rooster. It would be cruel of us to make him live in pain." All the kids sadly nodded. Nora and Sadie were crying. Wade continued to stare at his rope…his fingers running over the ridges.

"He could go into surgery and they find the damage is too extensive and put him to sleep there or, they can fix as best they can and hope it eliminates the pain. Even with the surgery, he may still need to be put down."

"Did you vote? Is he going to have surgery?" Grace asked nervously.

Wade looked up at his dad, his eyes wide and hopeful.

"There wasn't much to vote on," Aunt Dru spoke. "We would never put him down without at least trying everything possible." She looked at Grace. "Yes, he will have surgery."

"When?" Grace asked excitedly.

"Well, that's up to Wade," Aunt Dru said.

Wade's eyebrows went up in surprise. "Me?" He sat up in his chair.

"They have an opening this Friday or the Thursday after." His dad told him.

"Friday is my birthday." Wade reminded him.

His dad nodded. "That's why it's up to you. You now know the possibility that Rooster may not make out it out of surgery," he paused until Wade nodded. "Do you want to take the chance that Rooster is gone on your birthday?"

Wade thought about it very carefully, remembering the groan as Rooster stepped out of the horse trailer. Was he tolerating the pain like his dad had said? "I think we should do the best thing for Rooster and get him out of pain right away." Wade paused and took a deep breath. "One way or the other."

His dad nodded.

Reilly leaned over to Wade, "That's the right thing to do."

Wade smiled up at him and sighed. He was glad Reilly agreed with him. He looked around to see if everyone else did. The only person that didn't look happy was his mom.

"Can we go with him?" Sadie asked.

His dad shook his head, "That would be too many people."

Wade sat up in his chair and looked at his dad who had turned to him. "Me, Dad?" His voice cracked. He looked at Uncle Grayson who could confirm that he was good then back to his dad. "I was really good today and tried to be an adult. I will be good, I promise. Please

71

Dad?" Wade took a deep breath. "Rooster will need me…
you said I could in the barn when Rooster helped me…I
promise I will be an adult again…"

Wade stopped talking when his dad raised a hand to
stop the nervous fast talk.

"Yes, Wade. You did great today and we think you
will help keep Rooster's stress level down." Wade smiled
nervously. He saw his mom put her head in her
hands…she really didn't look happy.

CHAPTER SEVEN

"Stupid girls," Wade walked through the front door of the house and made his way to the kitchen. He looked out the back window and saw all the adults sitting around the tables on the deck. Out the side window, the girls were braiding all the horse's hair...even Rooster's and Dollar's. He'd told them not to, but they laughed and did it anyway. "Stupid girls." He repeated.

Wade was tired of the cast on his arm and tired of all the girls. Why did Reilly have to go home with his dad? Why did Matt have to go back to college? He was the only boy left at The Homestead. He turned in circles in the hallway, the lariat swinging around him. He didn't know what to do and felt grumpy, not wanting talk to anyone. He stopped and looked around. The door to the no-media room was open. It was the one place no one could watch TV or use their electronic games so hardly anyone ever went in there...unless one of the kids got in trouble.

Deciding it was a good place to get away from everyone, he walked down the hall. The girls wouldn't find him in there.

Wade walked in the room and past the gaming table to the left. There was a chair to the right of the door; hidden in the corner. It was big and fluffy with lots of pillows. He could sink into it and hide from the world, no one would find him there. Kicking off his boots he crawled up into the chair. The cast fit perfect up on the arm of the chair and he sunk back into the pillows. The lariat lay across his lap. He traced the coil with his fingers, the ridges of the rope were rough on his skin but he liked the feel…it was mesmerizing…a deep breath…let it out and try to release the bad mood…he watched his finger…concentrated on the feel…another breath and he felt his body relax.

Wade lifted his eyes from the rope and looked around the big room. It had 3 couches and 4 chairs, lots of sitting room for the family. A large rock fireplace was on the wall that connected to the outside wall with all the windows. Over the fireplace was barb-wire that was looped and bent in the shape of the ranch T3E brand. Around it, were four large coils of wire, one for each generation of Taggers' that owned the property. His dad had told him the barb wire was from the original ranch fencing constructed by Wade's great-great grandfather.

On the wall, to each side of the fireplace, were large canvas prints of Mavis during a branding. The one on the left was Mavis walking next to his dad's legs; they were headed to work the cows and she looked like she was glaring at the cows. The canvas on the right was Mavis lying down looking up at his dad who was leaning down petting her head. They were awesome and Mavis looked great in them. They always made him think of her working the cows at the ranch.

Wade could see the adults outside sitting at the table talking about Rooster and sighed. He didn't want Rooster to be in pain but he didn't want the horse gone either. Tears threatened to fall when he thought of the night Angel died. Sadie was heartbroken and cried herself to sleep in Uncle Grayson's arms. He took another breath and tried to blow away the tears. He was tired of crying.

A movement out the window caught Wade's attention. His mom had stood up quickly and turned to the house. Her chair had fallen back on the deck. As his mom walked to the house, Aunt Leah picked up the chair and followed. His dad's head was back and he was looking up at the sky. Both Aunt Dru and Uncle Grayson were leaning on the table and talking to each other. They didn't look happy either.

Wade heard the back door open and footsteps quickly coming down the hall. Holding his breath, he hoped the footsteps would go past the door; they didn't. His mom walked in the room. He was about to say Hi when Aunt Leah walked in.

"What was that all about?" Aunt Leah asked his mom.

Wade debated whether to get up fast and leave or wait. Wanting to know if they talked about Rooster, he shrunk back in the chair and tried to disappear into the pillows.

His mom turned and glared at Aunt Leah. "You know exactly what it's about! They made the decision that Wade would go to WSU without discussing it with me. They made the decision about the horse without any input from us. The horse is Wade's and yet I have no say in what happens to it."

"Rooster is Wade's responsibility but he belongs to Tagger Enterprises," Aunt Leah corrected. "So the decision is between the three of them."

"Everything is between the three of them." His mom was almost yelling.

"Jordan, calm down."

"Why? I've been calming down for years and I'm tired of it." She turned her back to Wade, so he couldn't see how mad she was.

"Well, that's bull," his aunt walked farther into the room. "It's been a great life Jordan. There is no better life out there. I don't know what's up with you."

"I'm tired of being the outsider."

"The outsider?"

"In this whole family! Don't you feel it?" She turned back to his aunt. "There's those three and all their kids, then there's us."

Aunt Leah shook her head, eyebrows raised in surprise, "I have NEVER felt that way, so don't lump me into that. I love my husband, my kids, and the entire family. I am not a fifth wheel to anyone or anything."

"Then I guess I'm on the outside all by myself."

"You're putting yourself outside, Jordan."

"It didn't upset you when they hired Cora?"

It was Wade's eyebrows raised in surprise this time. What did this have to do with Cora?

"Since it had to do with part of what we do here, yes it did. But I support the decision completely. I love Cora and am thankful I don't have to work all day, then come home and have to feed this herd of a family."

"I love Cora too. But they should have asked us first."

Out the window, Wade saw Aunt Dru stand and head for the house.

"As I understand it, Dru brought it up to them and they both agreed, so what's the problem?"

His mom sighed, "Of all people, I figured you would understand."

"Well, if she doesn't, then maybe you can explain it to me," Aunt Dru walked into the room; her voice tense. "Attacking Scott like that was uncalled for, Jordan. HE made the decision about Wade going up for the surgery, not the three of us. He was fulfilling the promise he made to Wade in the barn the other night."

The room was quiet. Wade looked at his mom while silently wishing he had left the room. No 'almost ten years old' should have to witness this.

His mom glared at Aunt Dru.

"Jordan, this has been going on too long. You have to talk this out so we can get passed this." Aunt Dru pleaded.

His mom turned and faced her. She took a deep breath, "This is not what I wanted when I got married."

"What did you want?" His dad walked in the room behind Aunt Dru.

Wade hadn't seen him get up. He glanced out the window and saw Uncle Grayson still sitting at the table and staring towards the pasture where the girls were playing with the horses.

Without saying anything, Aunt Leah walked out of the room. Wade could hear her footsteps echoing down the hallway. He should leave too, but he couldn't get his legs to move.

"What did you want?" his dad repeated.

Wade could feel his heart pounding and hoped they couldn't hear it. He didn't want to be there.

"I wanted a husband and family."

"What part of that didn't you get?" his dad asked.

"I got a husband and his family. Not our family."

"You knew that they were part of who I am and part of the marriage. So what changed?" His voice was angry and confused.

"I became the afterthought."

"Since when?" he asked in disbelief.

"Since the beginning," she answered.

He shook his head. "We were fine until last spring when the horses came into the family. Are they the issue?"

Wade held his breath, how could the horses be the problem?

"The horses are not the issue," she said gruffly.

"Is it Cora?" Aunt Dru asked.

His mom glared at her again and didn't answer her.

His dad looked between the two women. "What about Cora?"

"When we announced that we hired her, I saw you and Leah exchange a look." Aunt Dru said to her.

"I thought you liked Cora doing the cooking." Wade's dad seemed as confused as he was.

"I do," she answered.

"I don't understand, Jordan." his dad sighed.

His mom walked over to the window and looked out; she saw Uncle Grayson and quickly turned around.

"It's now or never, Jordan," his dad stepped towards her. "You have to tell me what's wrong so I can fix it."

"You can't fix it," she responded angrily.

His dad rolled his eyes and shook his head. "Then what do you suggest?"

"I'm going to pack up the kids and move into town for awhile."

Wade's eyes opened wide and his heart raced. Before he knew what happened he stood up and yelled, "No!"

All three of them jumped and turned surprised faces towards him.

"Wade!" His mom gasped and walked over to him. "What are you doing here?"

"I was in here by myself when you and Aunt Leah came in," he took a step towards her, his heart pounding. "I don't want to go anywhere!"

"Wade…" she began.

"No!" he said again. "I don't want to leave. I don't want to leave those bratty girls, or the horses. I don't want to leave dad just because you do!" Wade was nearly yelling at her. His heart was racing with a mixture of fear of leaving and anger at his mom for wanting to leave.

"Calm down, it'll be OK," his dad whispered in concern and took a step forward.

Wade's mom knelt down next to him, "Please calm down." she pleaded.

He realized they were worried of another panic attack, "I'm OK." His breathing was fine; it was his heart that was scared.

"I don't want to go anywhere," Wade repeated looking between his dad and mom.

"You're not going anywhere," his dad said firmly.

His mom stood and faced his dad and aunt.

"Aren't you going to vote on that?" she glared at him.

"What does that mean?" his dad asked angrily.

"You vote on everything else! So aren't you going to vote on whether you take my kids away from me?"

"Are you listening to yourself, Jordan?" His dad yelled at his mom, then stopped and took a deep breath to calm himself down. "I am not taking the kids away from you. You were threatening to take them away from me and the family."

"The family..." she said sarcastically.

It sounded like she was cursing.

"Jordan," his dad waited until she looked at him. "What is the problem?"

She didn't answer.

"What is the problem?" he repeated.

"Just spit it out, Jordan," Aunt Dru pleaded.

His mom looked out at Uncle Grayson, who was now talking with Aunt Leah, then turned and looked at Aunt Dru then his dad.

"I can't compete," she said bluntly.

His dad didn't say anything, his head tilted to the side like the dogs do when they are confused.

"I don't understand," Aunt Dru said.

"I feel like an outsider when it comes to this family," his mom's voice was shaking.

Aunt Dru looked over at his dad who was still just staring at his mom. Wade looked up at his mom because he was confused too.

"Since when?" Aunt Dru asked.

"Leah and I should have been consulted before hiring Cora," she said flatly.

"So it wasn't the horses, it was Cora?" his dad asked.

"I love Cora." his mom added quickly.

"But you didn't want us to hire her?" Aunt Dru looked frustrated, her neck was turning red…that only happened when she was getting mad.

"Hiring her was fine, but Leah and I should have been consulted," she said curtly.

"She was hired on by Tagger Enterprises," Dru argued. "So it was put up for a vote between the three of us, like everything else is that involves the company."

"It involved the responsibility of Leah and me, so we should have been included in the conversation," his mom replied.

"It wouldn't have changed the outcome," Aunt Dru reminded her impatiently.

No one spoke for a few minutes. Wade shifted his weight from one foot to another. It seemed like they forgot he was there.

"What did you mean you can't compete?" His dad finally spoke. Wade thought his voice was very soft compared to the tension in the air. He looked up at his mom. She was looking at his dad with angry eyes.

"I can't compete with the three of you," she answered tersely.

"You feel like you are competing with us?" his aunt asked, her voice raised an octave in confusion.

"I feel like everything I do, or want to do as a family, I am competing with the relationship between the three of you," his mom paused. "I wanted to marry Scott, not all three of you."

"You knew they were part of the deal when I asked you to marry me," his dad said.

"Yes, I did," she admitted. "But I didn't think it would become a competition between our relationship and the relationship between you three."

"We've been married for over 13 years, Jordan," his dad pointed out. "Why is this an issue now?"

"I guess it's been building," she answered, her voice still angry. "But when you hired Cora, without talking to us, it just showed how it was going to be forever."

"You want us to fire her?" Aunt Dru asked in angry disbelief. Wade just about yelled again but his mom answered before he could.

"Of course not," she said.

"Then what do you want?" his dad asked.

"I wanted that job," his mom finally replied.

"What job? Cora's?" His dad asked in disbelief.

"Yes," she answered.

"Why didn't you say something?" he asked looking confused and frustrated.

"Because I didn't think it was an option," she crossed her arms in front of her.

"Jordan," his dad took a step towards her. "Why didn't you say you didn't want to work at the paper mill?"

"I didn't say that," she turned away from him and looked towards the fireplace.

There was silence in the room again. Wade looked at his dad and aunt to see if they understood what his mother was saying, because he sure didn't. They looked just as confused as he felt.

"I am so confused right now," his dad finally said. "You wanted the position we gave to Cora but you don't want to quit your job?"

His mom still didn't look at them, "Yes."

"You couldn't do both," Aunt Dru pointed out.

"I know," she agreed.

"You know Tagger Enterprises is self-sufficient," his dad said and his mom nodded. "You don't have to work; you've known that all along. Your job has always been your choice."

"I know," she glanced back at him.

"Then what do you want Jordan? I am not going to tell you that you have to quit your job, or keep it. It's your choice." He said again.

"I love the people I work with. My job and the company are great," she started. "But I want to be more to this family and not feel like I'm competing against the three of you."

"I don't understand the competing part," Aunt Dru said. "There is no competition."

"Yes there is," his mom was frustrated again and Wade was confused. This adult stuff was hard.

"What do you see as competition?" his dad asked.

"I want to have what you three have," she yelled. "I want that bond, I don't want to compete against it."

"You do not want the bond that my brothers and I have," Aunt Dru said stiffly.

"Yes, I do Dru," Wade's mom glared at his aunt. "How can you stand there and tell me that I don't want what the three of you have? I want that bond, that strong of a relationship."

"There is no comparing our relationship to your relationship," Aunt Dru told her, taking a step forward. "There is no competing because it's not the same."

His mom started to say something but his aunt continued, "You don't want the bond we have, no one does. Your relationship is between the two of you, built on love." Dru waved her hand to point at his parents.

"It grew from love and is shared with the family; born of that love," Aunt Dru glanced at his dad and out the window at his uncle. "We were born as brothers and sister…but you have no idea what we went through to become the friends and partners we are now." The redness moved from her neck to her cheeks and her eyes were glaring at his mom, "You have no idea what it is like to be riding your horse on the best ride of your life one moment, and five minutes later have your whole world torn from you. In a blink of an eye you're part of a happy family, then BAM, you're an orphan." Her voice quivered.

"You have no idea what it feels like to cry in agony until you can't see or breathe. You feel like you're falling in a hole of despair with no way out. You have no idea what it's like to hold onto each other so hard that you begin to bond in a way that no one should ever have to," She paused to take in a deep breath. "I was drowning in agony in the barn the night of the funeral, and the only things that pulled me out, were the hands and love of my two brothers. It took all three of us, *together*, to have the strength to pull ourselves out of that hole and emerge from that barn. We knew when we dried our tears and walked out, that we only had each other, hearts and souls. There would be no one, besides the three of us, who would know the agony that we were feeling. " she paused, her voice had been shaking.

"Your relationship is built on love," she looked over at her brother. "Ours was built on family but bonded with the need to survive."

When she stopped, the room was eerily silent.

While Aunt Dru was talking, his dad had walked up beside her and taken her hand. She had tears sliding unchecked down her face and his dad was fighting hard not to let his tears fall. It's not right that Wade should be seeing his dad like this. Wade looked up at his mom and saw she was crying too. Then to his surprise, Wade's hand was reaching to wipe away the tears rolling down his own cheeks.

Aunt Dru wiped her face with her sleeve.

"I love you with my heart and soul Jordan," his dad said, the emotion made his voice crack and his eyes were anguished. "I don't give that love lightly because I know what it is like to have it ripped away," he looked at his sister. "No one can change or expect the relationship I have with Dru and Grayson to change. We have a bond that runs thicker than the blood we share in our veins," he paused and looked back at his wife. "I would not have survived without them."

His eyes dropped to look at Wade then back up at Jordan. "I don't want that type of bond with you. I want to be man and wife; the same way I felt the moment I met you, " he sighed, "If that isn't enough anymore…then I can't give you more. You have to decide if that bond is enough for you. It's your choice."

His dad left the room. Wade nodded at Aunt Dru when she looked down at him then followed her brother. He stood there not knowing what to do or say, so he just took his mom's hand and squeezed it. She had quit crying but didn't move or say anything either, she just squeezed back.

CHAPTER EIGHT

Wade sat at his bedroom window and looked at the lights of the city. His mom had left right after the argument. She had hugged him tightly and apologized to him that he had to witness the fight. After saying she loved him…she left.

"Why can't she just stay?" he mumbled to himself.

The moon was bright enough he could see the horses grazing in the pasture. For some reason, no one had put them back in the barn for the night. Nora, in her pajamas, walked in and sat down next to him.

"They look like ghosts out there," Nora leaned her head against the glass. She twisted her head to look at him, "Are you sad?"

"I wanted mom to stay." Wade mumbled; his shoulders slumped in defeat.

Nora sighed, "I don't know why she had to leave."

He didn't tell her about the conversation he witnessed. It wasn't his story to tell…he wasn't really sure whose it was…his Mom's…Dad's? There would be no good reason to tell Nora what happened anyway…it would make her just as sad and worried as he was.

"No matter what happens," Nora punched his shoulder trying to make him smile, "We'll always have each other."

His frown deepened; she made him think of Aunt Dru's story about the night of his grandparent's funeral. Wade's eyes started to tear up again.

"I'm not that bad!" Nora punched him harder. He lowered his eyes; willing the tears to go away.

"OK," she stood and headed for the door. "Let's go play with the horses."

"In the dark?" Wade hesitated, but when she disappeared down the hallway, he ran to catch up even though he knew they would get in trouble if someone found out.

Nora lifted her fingers to her lips to shush him. He walked on tip toes behind her. When they got to the top of the stairs and looked down, no one was there and they couldn't hear anyone either. Slowly they made their way down and looked out the back. Their dad, Aunt Dru, and Uncle Grayson were sitting on the back porch so they went to the side door. There wasn't a motion detector light out that way that would announce their late night adventure.

Once out the side door, they ran quickly to the fence and sat quietly. When they were sure no one saw them, Nora helped him crawl through the fence towards the horses; they were in the pasture between the front of the house and the road. Nora and Wade talked quietly to the horses so they didn't spook them.

"I'm surprised you like it out here in the dark," Nora whispered to him.

Wade looked around and up at the moon. "It's not that dark," He answered, glancing at his cast.

Wade looked over at Nora who was smiling and petting the horses while walking through them. In her white pajamas she looked like a ghost again. He walked carefully through the horses so he didn't accidently hit them with his cast.

He walked slowly between each horse. They were so relaxed and calm, as they grazed, that he began to feel the same way. All the trouble and stress of the last couple days was starting to flow out of his arms and legs…he felt like he was floating. This was the best idea Nora had ever had. He walked through making sure he touched each of them. Little Ghost seemed to glow in the light, living up to his name. Scarecrow's blonde hair stood out in the moon, too. Arcturus' star shown like the bright star he was named after. The moonlight shone off the horse's black hair.

Wade and Nora were giggling softly when they heard a truck start. They froze and went silent. He stepped around Buttercup to see which truck had started. Nora came up behind him.

"It's dad's truck," Nora said without seeing it.

"How do you know?"

"I recognize the sound of it. Sometimes, I lay in bed at night waiting for their trucks to come home, so I know they're OK."

The lights shone down the driveway...they waited. Soon the front of the truck passed the side of the house which caused the motion detector light to turn on. The light confirmed Nora's statement; it was their dad's truck.

"Where do you think he's going?" Wade whispered staring at the truck slowly making its way to the road.

"Well, it's been a bad day for him," she said and Wade silently agreed. Nora really didn't have any idea just how bad.

Nora continued, "If he turns left, he's going to the ranch and if he turns right, he's going to town, probably to Mom."

As the truck slowly moved down the driveway, Nora took Wade's hand. "Please go right, please go right..." she started whispering. Wade felt all the stress and anxiety make its way back through his body. How could one left or right decision make so much difference in their life?

The truck was half way to the road when it stopped.

"What is he doing?" Wade whispered.

"I don't know," She knelt down between Buttercup and Harvey and pulled Wade down with her. They were still holding hands while staring at the truck.

A little light glowed in the cab, "It's his phone." Wade whispered. He felt like a spy.

The light went out and the truck started moving.

"Nora," Wade looked at his sister's face, which was lit by the moon, "I don't want them to get a divorce, I don't want it to change."

"I know…me neither," she put her arms around him and they stared intently at the truck; quietly willing it to turn right.

Wade knew it wasn't the same, but he understood Aunt Dru's talk about the brother and sister bond now. He knew that in this moment, as they watched their dad, that no matter if the truck turned left or right, he and Nora would be closer than ever.

Wade leaned into his sister, understanding that she would always be there for him. He promised himself to always be there for her, too. They watched as the truck stopped. There was no indication if he was going right or left, the light came back on.

"This is killing me!" Nora squeezed tighter.

The light went out.

The sound of footsteps came from behind them. They hunched down even further, wishing one of the horses would lay down so they could hide behind it. Their eyes never left the truck even when the noise of the gate opening reached them. Wade realized he was holding his breath and slowly let it out. Every muscle was tense as he listened to someone walking towards them, while watching their dad sit in the truck at the end of the driveway.

The truck started moving again; it turned right.

Wade's eyes widened as he realized his dad could be going to his mom. He looked at Nora and she was grinning back at him. Then, slowly, the smile faded as her eyes slowly moved above him. He turned and saw jean covered legs. His eyes moved up to see Uncle Grayson staring down at them with an amused look on his face. Instantly Wade knew that their dad had seen someone in the pasture with the horses and had texted their uncle; busted!

"Care to explain?" Uncle Grayson asked.

They stood quickly and reached out to pet the nearest horse.

"We couldn't sleep, so we came out to check on the horses," Nora smiled, her eyes darted to the lights of her dad's truck making its way up the road.

Uncle Grayson turned and watched the truck lights turn the corner into town. "I understand," he said softly. The three of them watched the tail lights disappear into the mass of lights from Lewiston.

Rufio came up behind Uncle Grayson and rubbed his head against his arm, indicating the horse wanted some attention so he turned and stroked the horse's neck. He moved to the next horse and did the same. He didn't say anything, so Nora and Wade went back to petting the horses. The three of them quietly wandered between the horses, Wade and Nora would giggle softly when a horse nudged them.

Under the moonlight, the three of them played with the horses until the horses started to ignore them again. Cooper had lain down next to the fence; he was so dark it was hard to find the horse. Nora knelt at his head and stroked his neck.

Wade watched his uncle walk between the horses. He didn't have his hat on, so his dark blond hair was shining in the moonlight as he stroked Scarecrow's long neck. Then he turned to the next horse. He seemed really relaxed as he was talking to Harvey. A wide grin spread across Uncle Grayson's face when Eli put his head over the man's shoulder and lowered its long neck and head to pull Grayson to the horse's chest. The girls called it a special horse hug.

Wade decided it was just as relaxing for his uncle as it is for him. He turned to Nora. She was watching Uncle Grayson too, with a relaxed happy smile.

Wade walked to Rooster and ran his hand down the horse's neck to his shoulder, down his sides and up and over the horse's rump. Almost all of the bones were now covered with muscle and fat. He walked a complete circle around him and stopped at his head. Rooster leaned his nose onto his side. Wade leaned into him trying to forget that he might be gone forever in two days. Taking a deep breath, Wade filled his lungs with Rooster's essence.

Uncle Grayson came up behind him and put a hand on his shoulder causing Wade to look up to see understanding eyes looking down. His uncle understood the turmoil he was going through which caused tears to sting the back of his eyes again. The emotions of the week raced through Wade as he wrapped his good arm around his uncle's waist and leaned into his side. His uncle's arm draped around Wade's shoulders and he squeezed tightly giving him his silent support and love. It was a moment that Wade would never forget.

"Let's head in," His uncle motioned for Nora.

The three of them quietly walked to the gate. The horses continued their nightly grazing as if having their people out in the dark with them happened every night.

"No more coming out in here in the dark," Uncle Grayson told them as they walked through the gate, "unless you invite me."

***

The next morning, at the breakfast table, neither Nora nor his uncle mentioned their midnight visit to the horses, so Wade didn't either. It would be their secret.

Cora was still sleeping, so Aunt Dru and the girls were making breakfast. It was Thursday, so the kids didn't have school that day or the next. Wade was happy that Jack had dropped Reilly off at the house to spend the day with the kids and horses.

There was no sign of his mother or dad.

Reilly and Wade were sitting at the table with Uncle Grayson.

"Are we going to take Rooster up to the hospital tonight or in the morning?" Wade asked.

"We'll take him in the morning," Uncle Grayson answered and picked up the lariat that Cora had given Wade. "This is a real nice gift."

Wade nodded and watched Uncle Grayson playing with the rope. His uncle was the best roper he'd ever seen. He never missed a cow during branding.

"Why did you quit competing in the rodeo?" Wade asked.

A memory filled smile spread across his uncle's face, "To go to college…then to take care of the ranch," he ran a finger around the coil and over the ridges, just like Wade did when Cora gave it to him. Wrapping his hand around the rope he swung it back and forth getting the feel for the rope. "Your dad and I had a lot of fun team roping and traveling from rodeo to rodeo. Aunt Dru was there too, running barrels."

"How come you never talk about it?" Grace sat at the table next to her dad; Sadie quickly joined them. They liked to hear stories from their parents past…it didn't take long for Nora to join them too. Helping Aunt Dru with breakfast was abandoned. They all sat quietly waiting for his uncle to tell stories.

"It just seems like a lifetime ago," he answered Grace. "It was done and over years before you came along."

"Did you win a lot?" Reilly asked.

Uncle Grayson nodded with a big smile that made his eyes shine, "We did, but that wasn't the most important part."

"What was?" Grace asked.

He smiled at her, "Just riding, chasing the steer, throwing the rope, and having fun." He grinned at Nora and Wade. "Your dad was the best partner ever. If one of us missed we'd shrug it off and figure we'd get the next one. That's probably why we won so much…because we put the fun first. You guys have seen on TV… team roping is really fast," he looked around at the kids. "World record time is 3.5 seconds," all the kid's eyes opened wide. "A good header only throws after two turns and a healer will be there in five or six."

"Did you and Dad do it that fast?" Nora asked.

Uncle Grayson shook his head. "No, we usually averaged around 6 seconds."

"That's still really fast," Wade said. His uncle smiled and nodded. "What about calf roping?"

"The record is just over 6 seconds and the best ropers are consistently around 7 seconds." He answered. "You definitely want a fast and experienced horse."

Uncle Grayson paused, "Every rodeo weekend started the same way," he told his entranced audience. "Your grandma would visit the horses as we loaded them into the horse trailer."

"Why?" Reilly asked.

Uncle Grayson smiled, "She would tell the horses to take care of her kids."

"Telling them to win?" Grace asked.

Uncle Grayson shook his head, "No, telling them to make sure we didn't get hurt."

"In team roping?" Nora looked surprised.

He nodded at her, "Oh yeah. Many horses tripped coming out of the box or, the steer would dart in front of them and the horse would trip over it, sending the rider flying or rolling on top of him," he leaned back in his chair. "We watched one girl start out of the chute and the rope barrier snapped and wrapped around the back legs of her horse. She and the horse went rolling. She stood up and just walked off. They came back later and had a great run."

"Sounds scary!" Nora shook her head.

"Did Grandma and Grandpa go to all your rodeos?" Sadie asked.

"Not all of them, but they made it to some," he continued to bounce and swing the rope. "They had the ranch to take care of."

"What horses did you use?" Nora asked. Wade glanced over at her. She was always thinking of the horses and not the rodeo.

Uncle Grayson grinned at her. "Scott had a horse called Abraham, a little buckskin like Eli. He could stop and turn on a dime, so he and Scott were the header."

"Who did you ride, Dad?" Grace asked, enthralled with her dad's story.

"I rode a couple different horses," he handed the rope back to Wade. "I always seemed to be training a new horse."

"Did you or dad ever crash?" Wade asked. Watching buck-offs and crashes on TV was always the best part.

"Couple times, but nothing bad," he leaned forward in his seat. "Worse I saw was a steer dart in front of the horse and try to stop. The horse went right over the steer, tripped then rolled, sending the heeler up in the air and down on both legs…bent them backwards."

The girls groaned and the boys smiled.

"Dang!" Wade cried out and touched his cast. "That must have hurt!"

"Carried him off on a stretcher," his uncle chuckled. Men have such a weird sense of humor. "He was back competing two months later in Walla Walla and won."

"Did you or dad break anything?" Nora asked.

"Not in the rodeo, but at the ranch," he nodded at Wade's casted arm. "We both broke our arms when we decided to ride a couple calves in the back pasture."

Wade looked down at his cast and frowned. Was his uncle going to ask him how he broke his arm? He glanced up at his uncle and was surprised to see him looking at Grace instead.

"At the same time?" Grace asked.

"Yeah, and both the left arm," his uncle's eyes shone with mischievous memories. "We challenged each other to see who could stay on the longest. So, at the same time, we slid off our horses and onto the calves," he laughed. "We didn't even get bucked off."

"Then how did you break them?" Sadie asked.

"Some really pissed off mama cows!" He laughed and all the kids joined him. "Both of them chased their wild babies down a hill and we jumped off to get away from the mad cows. We both hit rocks and broke our arms."

"What did Grandma and Grandpa say?" Grace laughed.

He leaned back in his chair, "Well, they sure weren't as mad as we thought they would be." Wade waited for his uncle to turn to him accusingly, but he didn't. He just continued looking at Grace and telling the story. "Grandma just loaded us in the truck and took us into the doctor."

101

"And Grandpa?" Sadie asked.

His uncle chuckled and glanced up at Aunt Dru. "He just called us idiots and said, 'Well, I guess you won't do that again.'"

Everyone laughed but Wade. He looked down at his cast then up at his uncle. It wasn't the same. His dad wouldn't laugh or just call him an idiot; he would hate him and not love him anymore.

"Dad?" Grace said and everyone turned to her.

"Yeah?" He leaned forward with his elbows on the table.

She glanced over at Reilly who nodded at her. "Reilly and I would like to team rope with Buttercup and Rufio," her dad raised his eyebrows in surprise. "Would you help us train them?"

"Mine too?" Sadie added. "Little Ghost and I can do breakaway roping. Please, please, please!"

Wade sat up straight thinking about Dollar and Rooster.

"I haven't trained a horse for rodeo in a long time kids." He answered.

"It couldn't have changed much," Reilly said. "Team roping hasn't changed much…besides getting faster."

Wade watched his uncle look around the table at all the kids. They all eagerly waited for his answer.

"I'm older now," Reilly added quickly. "And will help with the ranch more so you can have time for training. I'll ask Dad and Scott if they will train me with shoeing so I can help with that too."

"I'll help with the ranch too," Grace added. "Anything you need."

Aunt Dru leaned against the kitchen counter with her arms crossed in front of her, she watched the group closely. Uncle Grayson sat back in his chair and glanced over at her. She grinned at him, obviously amused by the conversation.

"Uncle Grayson?" Wade said quietly and his uncle looked over at him. "I believe these horses came into our life for a reason." He looked down at the lariat that started the conversation then back up at his uncle. "Maybe getting back to the rodeo is what the reason is for you."

Uncle Grayson smiled at him and nodded, "Maybe you're right, Wade."

"So you'll do it?" Reilly asked hopefully.

His uncle looked around at all the kids. "It's a lot of work," he warned them.

Before he had a chance to answer, Wade's mom walked through the kitchen door; his dad right behind her. They were both smiling.

Nora and Wade quickly glanced at each other then at their parents. Their mom went to Aunt Dru and hugged her. Wade felt the relief inside, he smiled up at his parents.

"So what's going on here?" His dad asked and came up behind Nora and Wade; he kissed them both on the top of the head.

"Your brother is about to agree to train our little herd of kids and horses to rope in the rodeo." Aunt Dru grinned.

His dad laughed. It was a really happy laugh that Wade hadn't heard in a long time.

"Well kids," he looked around at them. "you couldn't ask for a better trainer. He sure trained some great ones for us," he started to sit on one of the empty chairs. "Let me tell you about Abraham..."

CHAPTER NINE

Wade lifted the rope and twirled it the best he could. He couldn't hold the rope in his casted hand so he watched Reilly throw the rope again. The loop sailed high, and just as it looked like it would land over the top of its target, it just kept going and missed.

"Lots of work and lots of practice," Reilly grinned at him. Wade nodded.

They had put the plastic calf head in the end of a straw bale to practice roping. The calf head had been in the barn for years and they had occasionally pulled it out and played with it. Now they had a mission.

"Dad said he was going to buy us mechanical training calves. They even have one to pull behind the 4-wheeler." Wade told Reilly. "That way we can practice roping without wearing out the cows."

"I've seen them," Reilly swung the rope in circles over his head again then threw it towards their make-shift calf. It went high again. He grinned at Wade, "and I need one."

Wade laughed, "You, me, Grace and Sadie all roping, we're gonna need more than one." He glanced over his

105

shoulder and saw the girls walking towards them; lariats in hand. "Like right now."

Reilly looked over and saw them too. He looked back at Wade. "It's guy time."

Wade happily agreed and coiled his lariat and tucked it under his arm. They took off running behind the house to get away from the girls. They started laughing when they heard the girls yelling at them and ran faster around the side of the house and all the way to the front only stopping when they saw the horses in the pasture.

Wade looked at Reilly and nodded. He used his good arm and hooked it over the top rail of the fence. Reilly balanced him and gave him an extra push to get all the way over. Once Wade was over, Reilly crawled up and over and they ran for the island in the middle of the pasture.

Reilly opened the gate for Wade and they each sat on one of the benches that faced each other.

"Sometimes, I really get tired of hanging out with just girls." Wade grinned at Reilly.

"Just need some guy time," Reilly grinned back. He stretched out on the bench with his arms behind his head. Wade copied him.

"Reilly?"

"Yeah?"

"I turn 10 tomorrow."

"I know that."

"How long have you and your dad been with Tagger Enterprises?

"About seven years."

"So I was three."

"That's the math," Reilly laughed.

"I don't really remember life when you weren't in my life."

"Are you getting mushy Wade?"

"Sort of," he chuckled. He was staring up through the limbs of the large oak tree…most the leaves had already fallen.

"OK, I'll sit through this," Reilly teased. "consider it your birthday present."

Wade laughed, "I like Rufio and Cooper."

"Me too. They're going to be great roping horses." Reilly said. Then he turned towards him. "I'm really sorry about Rooster. I'll be thinking about him all day tomorrow. So you better call as soon as you know anything."

Wade nodded, "We all spent a lot of time with the horses. He's mine…but ours too…"

They turned and looked back up into the trees.

"I miss Matt," Wade said.

"Where'd that come from?" Reilly laughed. "We were talking about horses."

"Yeah," Wade sighed. "My brain has just been jumping all over lately."

"So what's the mushy stuff you wanted to say?"

"I just wanted you to know that, no matter what happens, you'll always be my brother."

Reilly didn't answer him so he turned to look at him.

After a few minutes Reilly spoke; "I remember when I first got here, you used to follow me around like a puppy dog."

"So…that hasn't changed." Wade giggled.

Reilly laughed, "But I remember thinking back how I needed to protect you like you were my brother. Our parents didn't even have to ask me to help you if something happened or they were busy; I'd just be there helping you."

Wade smiled up at the tree, "You and Matt have always been there for me…us guys sticking together."

Reilly's legs flew up in the air and he twisted and sat up, slamming his feet on the ground with a bang. Wade laughed and awkwardly repeated Reilly's move the best he could with the cast on his arm. They were facing each other.

When he looked over at Reilly his smile faded. Reilly was looking at him with a serious expression.

"What?" Wade asked.

"You're about to get your first big brother advice," Reilly warned him.

"What?"

"How did you break your arm?"

Wade felt the tightness in his lungs again. His hand quickly went to his chest. He grimaced from the ache when he looked at Reilly.

"You OK?" Reilly asked in concern and moved to the bench next to Wade.

Wade slowly took a couple breaths. He didn't breathe too deep because he didn't want to have another panic attack. He looked over at Dollar who was grazing quietly in the pasture in front of them. He watched the horse's mouth open and close and his teeth pull at the grass. Wade looked to Dollar's big soft brown eyes. Then he glanced to the back of the horse and watched the tail flick back and forth. His lungs quit hurting.

"You don't have to tell me HOW," Reilly started, "but can you tell me WHY you're scared to tell anyone how it happened?"

Wade looked at the ground and considered the question, "Promise you won't tell anyone?"

"If that's the way you want it," Reilly nodded, "A brother's promise." He stuck out his hand. Wade hesitated then finally reached out and shook it.

Wade looked up at Reilly then down to the ground. He knew Reilly would keep his secret. "Dad will hate me if he found out how I broke it and I don't want to lose my dad." His stomach felt ill for just saying that much. He felt like throwing up.

Reilly nodded and admitted, "I've felt that before, but not to the extreme you're feeling it. You're making yourself sick over it."

Wade remained quiet. He was willing himself not to throw up.

"Wade," Reilly waited until he looked at him before he continued, "the other night, when you had your breathing attack, I saw how scared and worried your mom and dad were."

The guilt hit Wade as if Reilly had physically punched him. His eyes closed and he groaned… his heart began to hurt again.

"No," Reilly said loudly. "Look at me." Wade opened his eyes and met Reilly's worried blue eyes. "I didn't say that to make you feel bad. I said it so you could know how much you mean to Scott and Jordan."

Wade nodded but didn't say anything.

"You should tell your parents what happened." Reilly said.

Wade shook his head. "I can't."

Reilly sighed. "Do you think that there is anything that I could do to make my dad hate me?"

Wade frowned. "No."

"Does my dad love me more than Scott loves you?"

Wade didn't answer.

Reilly moved back over to the other bench so they could face each other again.

"Remember what Grayson said this morning about him and Scott breaking their arms?" Reilly asked. Wade nodded. "He said that his parents weren't as mad as what they thought they were going to be."

"I know," Wade whispered.

Reilly's phone announced he had a new message. He read it and sighed, "Dad's on his way."

They sat quietly a few minutes.

Reilly stood up and started jumping up and down.

Wade looked at him like he was crazy, "What are you doing?"

"Getting rid of the bad mojo," he answered with a grin, "You can't be serious if you're jumping up and down."

Wade laughed and stood up to join him. They were still jumping when they saw Jack's truck stop at the end of the driveway.

Reilly went through the gate then turned around, "Wade, there is nothing you can do that would make your dad hate you," He started to turn then hesitated. "Except maybe murdering someone," he had a mischievous grin on his face. "You didn't murder anyone did you?"

Wade chuckled, "No."

"Well then, tell your dad what happened." He turned and yelled. "And that's your first advice from your big brother!"

He watched Reilly, rope in hand, run across the pasture and meet his dad at the lower gate, then watched as the truck made its way down the road and round the turn to town. He lay back down on the bench with his good arm behind his head. All he could hear was the horses walking around and eating. Every once in a while a car would drive by.

He heard his mother calling out to him so he sat up, grabbed his rope that had fallen to the ground, and slowly moved over to the gate. As he started to push the gate open he looked up and saw Monty standing on the other side staring at him. He froze, fear gripping his heart. Why was his dad's horse here? He'd never seen him off the ranch. Wade felt his heartbeat getting faster...it was pounding in his ears. With shaking hands he slowly closed the gate, keeping the fence between them, but trapping Wade in the pasture island.

He didn't move anything but his eyes as he looked for the other horses. He could only see Eli, Buttercup, Cooper, Arcturus, and Trooper, so he slowly turned his head. Monty took a step towards him, he froze again. Wade's pulse was racing and his breathing started to increase. He took a deep breath and slowly let it out trying to stop a panic attack; no one was around to help him.

Wade took a step back away from the gate and Monty came running at him. Terror took over and he began walking backwards as fast as he could; he tripped on one of the plants and landed on his back. The big grey horse hit the fence chest first; his eyes staring right at Wade. Wade sat very still hoping Monty would leave.

The horse took a few steps backward then rammed the fence again. Wade stood up and ran to the far end of the island. Monty followed him snorting wildly, throwing his head in the air causing his mane to fly wildly; his eyes glowing.

"Stop!" Wade yelled at the horse as his panic heightened. He looked over at the house, someone on the front porch. It was his mom. "Mom!" He screamed. She turned away and walked in the front door.

Monty began ramming the fence next to him which made Wade's chest start to hurt again. His hand grasped at his shirt trying to pull it away to make more room to breathe. He ran down to the other side of the island. "Go away!" He screamed again and started gasping for breath in big gulps. He looked around desperately trying to find something for protection. Monty rammed the fence again and Wade could see the top rail crack. The fear began bubbling out of his stomach and up his throat. The next push caused the rail to break in half and fall slowly to the ground. The horse stopped and stared at him. Wade knew that Monty could get to him now. He'd seen the horse jump brush and fallen trees that high.

He tried to yell but vomited instead, making him gag and fall to his knees. Monty took a step backwards and the horse's head swung to the left. Wade looked in the same direction, "No!" he tried to scream. Monty was looking at Rooster who was grazing peacefully unaware of the monster of a horse aiming for him. Wade forced himself to stand up and leaned his head back and took a slow deep breath. He would have to calm down to save Rooster. Lowering his head, Wade looked for Monty.

The horse was prancing around wildly until he suddenly stopped and reared up on his back legs. He looked huge…a monster of a horse. Monty lunged forward, flying in the air directly at Rooster. Wade screamed and ran for the fence slamming into it then falling backwards on the ground. Everything went black.

Wade sat up breathing so fast his whole body was tingling, his head back in the fog. He looked up in time to see his dad jumping over the fence Monty had just rammed and his mom running behind him. Nora was running behind her. Wade looked around trying to find Monty and Rooster.

Rooster and the other horses were standing at the fence watching him.

He had fallen asleep on the bench and was having a nightmare. He lifted his arms as his dad grabbed him. His dad's whole body was shaking. His mother opened the gate and ran to their side, wrapping her arms around them; tears streaming. Nora quickly joined them and was pulled into their family hug.

No one spoke; they just held each other tightly.

Wade realized they were all too scared to speak. He must have screamed when Monty attacked. He turned his head and saw Rooster. Monty wasn't attacking Rooster…Rooster was OK. He tried to get his breathing to slow down by watching the horse.

His arms were wrapped around his dad's neck, cast and all so he could feel his dad's heart racing. Wade took a few deep breaths to relax then concentrated on his dad's heartbeats; they both started slowing down.

Then he thought of Reilly's brotherly advice.

"I didn't murder anyone, Dad." Wade whispered.

"What?" His dad's arms relaxed but didn't let him go.

"Reilly said you would love me no matter what, unless I murdered someone." He explained.

"Reilly started this?" His mom asked.

"No," Wade leaned back to look at them. Their faces were still tense and now a little confused. "Well, sort of."

"Wade?" His dad said softly.

Wade looked up at him. "Yeah?"

"Reilly is right."

CHAPTER TEN

Holding onto the corner of the cattle ramp, Wade stood on the wood fence; stretching as high up on tippy toes as he could. He tilted the cowboy hat so it shielded his eyes from the sun. The cows had started coming up over the hill a few minutes ago. So at any time now, he should see the riders. Wade looked to his right and saw his mom and Jessup.

Jessup was one of his favorite people ever. He had started working at the ranch before Wade was born. After The Stables were built, Aunt Dru started working more at new business than at the ranch, so they needed a new foreman at the ranch. Jessup had broken his hip at the ranch where he worked before Tagger Enterprises, and that ranch wouldn't hire him back when he healed. The Tagger Trio had hired him as fast as they could. They didn't want someone else to get him.

Wade didn't know how old Jessup was, but he knew he was younger than Cora…they told him that much. Jessup walked with a limp, which Wade thought was cool…it made the older man look like he came out of a

John Wayne movie. If he couldn't ride with his dad, Wade always wanted to ride with Jessup.

Wade looked behind them and saw Aunt Dru and Aunt Leah. Reilly and Grace were next to the horse trailers talking. All of the cows that their groups had gathered were already standing and mooing in the large corral and out in the pasture. He couldn't see Sadie and Nora. The group at the corrals were all waiting for the men to bring in the rest of the herd. They had ridden deep into the canyon where it was too dangerous for little kids to ride.

Mavis had helped with his group and Bart ran with Aunt Dru and Aunt Leah. The dogs did the hard work of chasing the cows out from under brush and down from steep hill sides where the riders couldn't get to.

Wade turned his attention back to the incoming bunch of cows. He stretched higher, wanting to get that first glimpse of his dad. The calves were running around trying to find their mothers. The moms were mooing… trying to call their babies. It was so loud Wade could barely hear himself think!

Wade looked down at the fence he was standing on. It was 2 inches wide and he knew he could walk on it to the other side…maybe then the riders could be seen. Slowly putting one foot in front of the other and balancing with his arms he walked across; the last few steps he finished quickly. Hearing his mom yelling, he glanced over, waved and turned back to the cows. She was going to tell him to stop walking on the fence, so he pretended he couldn't hear over the mooing.

There they were! His dad, Jack, Matt, and Uncle Grayson were riding behind the cows. Wade bounced on the fence in excitement. "Look at them," he whispered. They were wearing their cowboy hats and their chaps over their legs. It wasn't too cold, but they had long shirts on and his dad and uncle wore their black vests…they looked like they were in a movie.

He watched their every move, "I want to be there." Wade said out loud.

"Where?" Sadie said from behind him on the ground.

"Out there with dad and the men," he answered without moving his eyes from the riders.

"You will someday," she encouraged.

Suddenly a cow bolted from the back of the herd and headed up the hillside. His dad and Monty took off at a gallop after it. They ran up above the cow then down in front of it to push it back into the herd. *It was magnificent!*

As his dad made his way back down to the riders, Matt, Jack, and Uncle Grayson turned in their saddles to face him and started clapping; giving him a round of applause for his performance.

Wade laughed. He couldn't hear them over the loud cows but he knew they were joking and laughing and he just wished he was there.

He heard someone ride up next to him, "I'm going in to help Cora with dinner," it was his mom. Wade kept his eyes on the riders but nodded. "Do you want to ride with me?"

"Nah, I'm OK, Mom."

"Are you sure?"

"It's OK," he assured her without looking.

He didn't hear her go; just watched the cowboys pushing the cows. The corral was nearly bursting with all the cows that were in it already. It was a lake of red and black backs.

Wade quickly looked around and saw that only Reilly and Aunt Dru were still there, off their horses and ready to shut the gates. Everyone else had headed up to the house for dinner. He couldn't believe they didn't want to see the riders come in, it was one of the best parts of the day.

Before his dad could see him, Wade quickly fence walked back over to the ramp.

"Wade, knock it off!" He heard his dad over the mooing of the cows. Busted!

Wade turned and grinned at his dad like nothing was wrong. His dad rode up beside him, wrapped his arms around Wade's knees, and pulled him over his shoulder. Still on horseback! Wade screamed with laughter.

"Dad!" Wade had to brace his hands on Monty's rump, his feet high in the air over his dad's head.

"You said you wanted to ride Monty today," his dad laughed and walked the horse back to where Matt, Jack, and his uncle were.

"Yeah, but not upside down and backwards." Wade laughed.

"That's the way you ride all the time," Matt teased.

Wade just laughed as his dad walked Monty closer to Matt, who helped him get turned around and sitting behind his dad. Wade wrapped his arms around his waist tightly and looked around. Aunt Dru and Reilly had shut the gates to the pasture and were looking over the cows. Reilly was standing next to Jack who was still mounted on his horse.

Uncle Grayson sat quietly looking at the cows.

"Wade," his dad had turned in the saddle trying to see him.

"Yeah, Dad."

"Promise me you will stop walking on the fence tops."

"OK, Dad." Wade looked over at Matt who had lifted his cowboy hat off his head and was wiping the sweat from his forehead. He smiled at Wade, "Want me to lead your horse back?"

Wade nodded, he may be "almost ten" but he still liked riding with his dad on Monty.

"I'm hungry, I hope dinner's ready." Matt hollered over the noise of the cows as he untied Wade's ranch pony and led him in the direction of the house; Uncle Grayson and Jack falling in line behind him. Aunt Dru and Reilly quickly mounted their horses and followed.

That left just Wade and his dad coming up the back.

"Can I ride him today?" Wade asked his dad once they got away from the loud cows.

"Not today son. He's a bit riled up after chasing cows. You need to grow a little more. He needs a strong rider."

"OK," Wade sat quietly behind his dad as they made their way up the road that led to the house. Monty was relaxed and walking with ease. His dad barely moved his hand to turn him left or right so Wade was convinced he could ride him.

Wade turned and looked back at the corral full of cows, "Are we going to work all of them tomorrow?" It was time for pregnancy test, shots, and separating out the cows that would be sold.

"We'll get them all done, but it will be late when we finish and head home."

"Headed home on Saturday?" Wade was surprised. "I thought we weren't going home until Sunday."

"Seems, someone has a birthday coming up and presents have to be bought and party arrangements need to be made."

"Well...that's a pretty good reason if you ask me!" Wade said happily. He glanced over and saw a new trail cut through the trees. "Where's that trail go?"

His dad glanced over. "Jessup must be working on something." He turned Monty to head up the trail instead of the road.

"Oh cool!" Wade grinned. He was off on an adventure with Dad.

He sat quietly enjoying the motion of the horse. Every once in a while he bent sideways around his dad to see where the trail was leading.

"Can you tell where it's going?" Wade asked.

"It looks like it's going to meet up with the other road. Probably a shortcut so you don't have to go all the way up to the house and around the big corner to move between the barn and the corrals."

"That's a great idea."

The trail ended between the barn and the house. They turned and saw Matt and the other riders just coming into the driveway.

"That's quite a shortcut." Using his dad's arm he swung off Monty.

His dad agreed as the other riders came up wanting to know how they got there so quickly. Wade walked proudly next to his dad as they made their way into the house for dinner.

***

After a full day of school, the drive to the ranch with Cora, and riding all afternoon, the kids were tired; except for Wade. Even the parents were tired. By nine o'clock the whole house was asleep except Wade and Jessup. Jessup had driven to Andy's house to pick up supplies for the next day.

Wade lay in bed looking around the bunkhouse. It was just one large room with eight sets of bunk beds placed along the walls, four on each side. The lower bunk was larger than the upper bunk, so the adults slept in the lower beds and the kids in the upper beds. Dressers were placed against the wall in between the bunks. Matt was on the bottom portion of the bunk bed that Wade was in. There was a small kitchen area at one end of the building and a bathroom at the other end, by the door. It was always fun to sleep in the same room as everyone else. Jessup and Cora were the only ones that slept in the two of the three bedrooms in the ranch house.

Wade sat up in bed and looked around. Light snoring echoed throughout the room. Bart was curled up on the foot of Matt's bed and Mavis was curled up on Nikki's bed. Looking outside the window, the moon was almost full. Wade could see the outline of the barn on one side of the bunkhouse and on the other side he could see the roof of the house.

There was a window next to the bunk bed Wade was in so he quietly slid out of bed to stand at the window and looked at the sky. The moon lit up the house and the little white fence that created a yard around it. Trucks were lined up in front of the house.

"I bet you can see the stars real good from the back of the truck." He crawled back up on the bed and lay quietly. His legs started getting restless and he had to keep moving them so they didn't itch. Finally, giving up and climbing back down the bunk ladder, he walked carefully down the row of beds to the door. It was still warm out, so the brown hoody he was wearing was warm enough. All their boots where lined up along each side of the door. It took him a minute of searching to find his own boots then tucked them under his arm before he slowly turned the handle of the door. There was no sound as it opened. One last look in the bunkhouse; there was no movement from anyone except Bart. The dog jumped off the bed and trotted to him then out the door. Wade glanced around the room one more time and then slowly slid out the door and closed it carefully.

He took a few steps away from the door and slid on the boots then walked around the corner of the house to see where Bart went. The dog had lifted his leg on the nearest tree.

Wade walked over to the trucks intending to crawl into the back of one of the them and watch the stars from the top of the tool box. Bart followed right behind him, but when Wade stopped the dog kept going.

"Bart!" Wade whispered as loudly as he could. The dog just kept trotting down the road. He was headed to the corrals where the cows were penned in the large enclosure and the horses in a small corral next to them. He took off running behind the dog.

"Matt and Dad are gonna be mad if you get hurt, Bart." He mumbled after the dog.

The dog didn't care, so Wade continued to run after him until he got to the big corner that led to the corrals. It was so dark he couldn't see the corrals in the distance so he turned to look at the bunkhouse. Wade was too far away and couldn't see it anymore, so he continued down to the corral...he needed to get the dog back.

When he arrived at the corrals he stopped and looked around for the dog, who was nowhere to be seen. He walked over to the horse corral and climbed on the gate; he sat quietly and stared up at the twinkling stars. The large bright moon lit the area around the corrals. He looked back up the road to the corner that led to the house. There were no lights; it looked like a black oasis. The outline of the trees could be seen because the sky was so light. If it hadn't been for running after Bart, he wouldn't have been brave enough to walk through the dark night to the corrals.

Wade felt a nudge on his back. He jumped and turned quickly only to see the horse that Jack was riding standing next to him. The horse was curious about Wade so he reached out and petted it between the ears. The horse shook his head, not liking his ears played with. Wade chuckled then looked around the group of horses. They were so tired there was still hay in the feeders and the horses were either lying on the ground or standing along the fence sleeping.

Wade looked for Monty and found the grey horse standing on the opposite side of the corral, head down, and eyes closed. Wade climbed higher on the fence. The cattle ramp was to his right and the posts were high enough for him to use as a brace as he stood on the fence. Out of habit, he turned to look to see if anyone was watching him, then laughed at himself.

He climbed the fence and stood high above the horses feeling like the king of the cowboys. He wanted to get over to Monty so he looked around the corral and planned his path; without touching the ground of course…what kind of an adventure would that be? He needed to jump from one side of the cattle ramp to the other, then swing his leg back to the fence and pull himself up. From there he could stand and fence walk over to the corner of the corral to Monty. There was a large four post brace in the corner and he could stand comfortably to see the horse.

Wade leaned back, holding the side of the cattle ramp, and jumped to the other side. Both hands wrapped around the top of the ramp holding him up. His legs dangled free. Swinging his legs over to the fence and catching his boot on the rail, he walked his hands across the top of the ramp to get his body all the way over. When he got there, it took all his strength to pull himself all the way on top of the fence. He stood. "Yes!" Wade grinned; proud of his accomplishment.

Now for the fence walk…he braced himself with the tall ramp post and took a first tentative step. He began to fall to the right and grabbed the post to keep from falling. The horses were in the corral to his left and there were cows to his right. A few cows were black with white faces; all the others were either solid black or solid red. He couldn't see the cows well, but every once in a while he would see a flash of white from their face.

"Don't fall," he said to himself and took another step; all good, so he took another, then another. Now, he was too far away from either side to grab anything for balance, so he began to walk faster. He started to fall to the right, and balanced himself by leaning hard to the left and walking faster to make it to the four post brace. "Yes!" He shouted and stood proudly on the corner post.

Bart barked, Wade turned quickly to see if he could see the dog…too quickly. He felt himself going backwards and turned to try to catch the fence. He was falling into the cattle corral! He lunged to catch the fence and missed, there was no way he could protect himself and looked to see where he was going to land; the metal cattle squeeze chute was under him. It had bars over the top and side and was used to catch and hold the cows while they were doctoring them.

Wade put his left arm out to try to catch himself on the chute, he grabbed for a bar, but missed and fell passed it. His arm caught between two of the bars as his body hurtled to the ground. A scream escaped when he felt the arm catch then break; shearing pain ran from his upper arm into his shoulder. He hit the ground, landing on his back. The force freed his arm from the chute but caused it to slam into the ground painfully. He lay stunned. The pain was so bad he couldn't even cry.

Then he heard them…the scream had scared the cows. They were beginning to mill around faster and faster; closer and closer. The ground under him started to vibrate. Fear shot through his stomach as a large calf appeared with its mother right behind it. She stopped and stared at him. Streams of snot were running out of her nose and her eyes looked frightened. More cows came up behind her.

Wade's mind went to Charlie, in his favorite movie *The Cowboys*. When Charlie went down into the cows to get his friends glasses, he spooked the cows and they trampled him to death. Wade could see them wrapping Charlie in a blanket and lowering him into the grave.

Terror screamed out of Wade, causing the cows to start moving around each other. The cow that had stopped and stared must have thought he was going to hurt her calf. It charged him. Despite the horrid pain shooting through his arm, Wade turned onto his stomach and tried to crawl away from the cow. The ground shook under him…he closed his eyes and prepared to be trampled. A loud crash sound echoed through the night…it was louder than the cow's hoof beats…then silence. All he could hear was animals breathing.

When the cow didn't hit him, Wade slowly turned his head to see where she went. The scared cow was so close, the snot was dripping only inches away from his face. Her breath pushed its way down the top of Wade's head and down his back. He lay frozen; not knowing what to do.

Another loud crash rang out. The cow shook her head and turned to leave. Then another crash! The cow swung around to run away; she bucked with a twist and a kick- out with her back legs. A back hoof landed on the lower portion of his already injured arm, breaking it too. He screamed again as another loud crash echoed and the cows moved away.

Wade began to cry from the fear and the pain. He knew his arm was broken; twice. When the tears finally stopped, he remembered the loud crashing. What had caused it? Flipping his head around in the direction of the noise; his eyes widened in horror. Monty was standing at the fence...his chest bloody from where the horse had slammed against the fence. The top rail was broken and the second rail was cracked. He'd hurt Monty. His dad was going to kill him! Wade crawled to the fence dragging his broken arm along the ground.

Monty was leaning over the broken fence. When Wade got to him, the horse's breath ran down his back as the horse nudged his ear.

"Monty, I'm sorry," Wade cried. He looked at the horse's wounds and saw two deep gashes running across the whole chest, blood dripping. "I'm so sorry."

Wade lay quietly with Monty standing over him. He didn't know what to do. It wasn't very late and no one would be getting up for six or seven more hours. He couldn't lay there that long. He looked down at his arm but couldn't really see anything, but there was a sensation of something running down the inside of his sleeve. Wade guessed it was blood...now he and Monty were both bleeding.

There were bears and mountain lions on the ranch and he knew they were attracted to blood...they could smell it from long distances. He remembered seeing the half eaten calf from a cougar kill. It made him sick to his stomach to think of Monty that way. Wade needed to get help for Monty.

CHAPTER ELEVEN

With his right arm, Wade pushed himself into a sitting position; streaks of pain ran up the arm and into the shoulder. He cried out making Monty bounce his head up and down. Wade took a deep breath and let it out slowly. His mind had to be clear to be able to get help for the horse. Reaching up with his good hand he petted Monty on the nose.

"Thank you, boy." Monty had saved him from being trampled to death like Charlie. The arm began to throb. He needed to get back to the house before the pain took over and he couldn't move.

There was no way he could go over the fence. He would have to crawl under the bottom rail. One more pat on Monty's nose and he rolled over on his knees to crawl under the fence to get out. His left arm dragged helplessly along the ground as he crawled to the fence. When he reached it, he lowered his body and dipped his head under the rail and used his right arm to pull his body under the bottom rail. Once through, he laid on his stomach to catch his breath. Sweat was running down his face and he could still feel the blood trickling inside the arm of the hoody.

Wade looked up the road to the house, seeing nothing but black…but he knew how to get there. He needed to move. Should he crawl or try to get up and walk? He decided walking would be faster and pushed up with his good arm, which caused the broken arm to move forward. Shooting pains ran up the arm and across his back and he nearly passed out. Wade remained on his hands and knees until the searing pain subsided. He leaned up with his good arm grabbing the fence…again the searing pain when the arm fell to his side. He pulled up with his good arm and finally stood, leaning against the fence.

"Don't pass out." Wade told himself and held tightly to the fence rail. He felt dizzy and needed to vomit. Taking a deep breath…letting it out slowly then doing it again, the dizziness started to clear.

He looked up the road into the darkness that led to the house…fear and doubt racing through him. "I can't do it."

Tears pushed behind his eyes and his shoulders slumped. One of the horses whinnied softly, making him think of Monty and the blood dripping from the horse's chest. Wade could still feel blood dripping down his own arm. He thought of the cougar kill.

"*I have to do this*," Wade told himself, he lifted his shoulders and strengthened his back. "I have to. Dad will hate me if Monty dies."

He pushed himself away from the fence and tested letting go. He wobbled to the right, which caused his bad arm to swing painfully. He cried out as the pain ran through the arm and back again. He forced himself to remain standing when his knees wanted to buckle.

Once his head cleared, Wade took a step, then another, and another. He tried to ignore the pain that shot through his body with every step. Staring at the ground, concentrating on the dirt, he took a few more steps. Pause, take a deep breath, three more steps, then pause again. He heard the horses and cows moving around. "For Monty…" he told himself and took three more steps. "For Monty…" he repeated and took three more.

Wade's head began to fog again. He couldn't shake his head without jerking the arm, so he took a couple deep breaths and let them out again. It didn't help.

"Just keep walking for Monty," He said out loud and took another step. He stopped and looked up to see where he was. The corral was still visible behind him. He wanted to cry. It was going to take him hours to get to the house at that pace.

"I have to," Wade told himself and took another step then stopped. He remembered the short cut trail he and his dad had ridden; it would make it faster to get back to the house. Wade slowly walked to the side of the road where he had seen the trail. Not really sure where it was, he just kept walking, hoping to run into it. Finally, he saw the gap in the trees.

Wade looked up the road; the moonshine lit a portion of the road in front of him and also made the top of the trees visible. He turned and looked down the trail. The moon's light couldn't reach the trail through the trees; it was pitch black. The trail had been wide enough for two horses and was in a straight line. He knew he could do it… but it was so scary.

Wade's legs began to shake. He needed to start moving again. Looking between the two paths and thinking of Monty's bloody chest, he turned left and walked into the darkness, continuing to walk three steps at a time. He tried to imagine the path that they had followed. He kept walking, his head got lighter, and felt his knees wobbling again.

"For Monty," he whispered and concentrated on one step at a time.

A wave a nausea ran through his stomach and up into his head…making him dizzy; his feet began to feel heavier. Each step was slower…he barely had the strength to pick his feet up; they were dragging…making it that much harder to take another step. He knew he was going to fall so he stopped and tried deep breathing again. It didn't work. He tried another step but stumbled and fell to his knees. The broken arm jerked and the pain soared through him again; a cry of agony escaped.

Wade leaned forward and placed the good hand on the ground. His broken arm fell forward…hand dragging at his side. He tried crawling, but the movement of lifting the good arm, pushing it forward and dropping again to the ground caused even more pain. Laying on his stomach again he pushed with his feet and pulled with the good arm, he moved forward. Wade remembered seeing army guys in the movies crawl that way with both arms.

"I can do it," he said out loud. Continuing to crawl forward until his right hand landed on a rock, he realized he was too far to the side so he angled himself differently and kept moving.

The pain in the broken arm was easier to bear this way than dangling at his side. He continued to crawl. He looked up and saw complete blackness, so he put his head down and continued to push and pull himself along the trail. He visualized Monty's bloody chest and the cougar kill to motivate him to keep crawling.

When he stopped to rest, there was breathing behind him. Fear rushed through his body again and was about to scream when he felt the lick on his face…it was Bart. Wade wanted to cry in relief.

"Oh, Bart," he cried out loud.

Wade took a deep breath and continued to crawl. The dog walking along side of him seemed to give him a burst of energy. His left shoulder bumped into something and pain shot down his arm…his head swirled in fog and was scared he was going to pass out.

"I have to make it to the road." Wade told the dog. He looked up and had to blink twice. Seeing the tips of trees highlighted with the moonlit sky, he knew he had to be getting close to the end of the trail. He took a deep breath and continued. His broken arm had gone numb and only noticed it when it hit a branch or rock.

"What do I do when I get there?" he asked Bart. Dad was going to hate him. He had let Bart out of the bunkhouse, he had promised not to fence walk and yet he did it again and broke that promise. He felt the heaviness in his heart as he realized how disappointed his dad would be. He had always told Wade that a man should always keep his promise. Yet he broke his promise to his dad.

Wade continued to crawl as his head grew lighter and his heart heavier. The worst thing was…he caused Monty to get hurt and he was now bleeding and could be prey for a bear or cougar.

Raindrops touched his cheek. What else could happen?

Wade continued to crawl and adjust to the path as he hit things along the way. The raindrops came faster and heavier. Bart walked quietly next to him. His hand reached out and landed on gravel. He had made it to the road!

He looked up and could see the outline of the trees. Looking left, he could see the top of the barn. He was so close. Turning right toward the house and bunkhouse he continued to crawl.

More raindrops splattered on his face.

Wade's head was getting lower and lower to the ground. Each stretch of his hand was slower and slower. He couldn't get his arm to lift him anymore. "I'm so close." Wade cried as his eyes began to close. "For Monty." he whispered and tried again, but his arm wouldn't move. "I can't stop now." Trying again, nothing in his body moved. His eyes closed.

Wade could hear Bart barking beside him; barking over and over again. He tried again to open his eyes but they wouldn't open. The ground began to rumble but he had no idea what it was. In one last effort, Wade opened his eyes just enough to see lights coming at him. They stopped just before it reached him and a limping figure was coming towards him; it was Jessup.

Wade tried hard to say Monty but his mouth couldn't get the words out. Suddenly he felt a searing pain run up his arm and through his body as Jessup tried to move him. He cried out and everything went black.

***

Nobody had spoken while he told the story. Wade sat quietly and couldn't get brave enough to look at his dad. He was sure his dad hated him.

"Jessup started honking the horn to get our attention," his mom said. They were still sitting on the bench. Wade was tucked in his mother's arms and could see his dad across from him. Nora was wrapped in his dad's arms. "Bart was running frantically around you."

"We got you to the hospital as fast as possible," Nora added.

"You were so close to the house that we didn't even think Monty's injuries had anything to do with you," his mom continued. "The rain...then the wind started just after we loaded you in the truck. Jessup tried to follow your trail but he couldn't, so we had no way of knowing what you went through." She squeezed him tightly.

Wade kept his head down. His dad wasn't talking.

Wade turned and looked up at his mom's eyes.; they were so dark...almost black...and there was pain...worry...fear...and love. He had scared his family...hurt them...broke his promise...from the bottom of his heart, he spoke, "I'm sorry," he said with such honesty that more tears sprung to her eyes.

He turned to Nora and looked into her eyes, "I'm sorry."

She wrapped her arms around him and hugged him; when she sat back she held his hand tightly while the tears fell down her cheeks.

Wade still couldn't look at his dad…he knew the truth now…he was sure he hated him; Wade had caused Monty's injuries and promises were broken. Wade hadn't cried as he told the story but now, knowing he lost his dad, the tears streamed down his face and dripped onto his shirt; he didn't even try to wipe them away.

The four of them sat in silence for a long time.

His mom reached out and gently touched the side of his dad's face, but he still didn't move, his eyes looked across the pasture. Slowly, she moved out from behind Wade, kissed him on the top of the head and took Nora's hand.

"But Mom," Nora complained as she was led out of the island, leaving him and his dad alone.

Wade sat on the edge of the bench and stared at the ground. Even if he never spoke to him again, his dad needed to know that he was sorry for what happened to Monty.

He didn't look up but spoke as firmly as he could, "I'm sorry Dad, for breaking my promise…I promised I wouldn't fence walk and I broke that promise. I'm sorry for almost losing Bart and I am really sorry that Monty got hurt."

Wade stood and turned away to walk to the house.

"Wade," his dad's voice was so low Wade barely heard it. What was worse; he called him Wade, not Buddy. His heart started to hurt worse than it did all week. There was no painful lungs or panicked breathes, it was just a breaking heart. He took a deep sobbing breath that shook when he released it.

"Turn around," his dad said in a whispered voice. Wade did as he was told and turned around but he stared at the ground.

"Chin up and look at me."

Wade tried…he lifted his head but his eyes went closed because he didn't want to see the disappointment on his father's face.

"Wade, look at me."

With all his might, Wade forced his eyes open and looked at his dad.

He was still sitting on the bench, so their heads were at the same height. His eyes were sparkling from tears that hadn't fallen. There was no disappointment in his eyes.

"You," he started, but his voice cracked from emotion. He stopped and started again. "You are the bravest and strongest young man… What you went through …to help Monty…incredible. The strength to put yourself through the pain, to go into the darkness, and fight to continue…." His voice broke and a tear fell.

Wade stared in disbelief. "You don't hate me?" His heart raced in hope and desperation.

"Hate you?" His dad sounded surprised. "Never."

Wade took a deep breath and let it out slowly.

"Buddy, I am so proud to be your dad." His arms spread out and Wade ran into them. He called him Buddy! Wade hugged his dad as tight as he could.

After a few minutes his dad finally spoke again; "I'm just glad you didn't murder anyone."

Wade giggled.

CHAPTER TWELVE

Wade walked to the barn; he didn't want to be there when his parents told everyone how he broke his arm.

All of the Tagger Herd stuck their heads over the stall doors. Wade smiled; it was the best sight ever. No one had fed them yet because they were called to the house as soon as they had put them in their stalls. He looked at his cast, looked at the horses, then looked at the wheelbarrow.

"I'll give it a try," he said out loud to the horses.

Ten minutes later, Wade finally got the hay into the wheelbarrow and slowly maneuvered it into the barn. He was just able to balance the handle with his casted hand to get a half load of hay at a time. He had broken into a sweat by the time the last horse was fed.

Grabbing a brush, he made his way to the stall with Rooster and Dollar. The horses had put on enough weight that the inside stall wasn't big enough for them to move around so the door to the outside section of their stall was left open. Which meant it was getting chilly.

"Wish I'd brought a coat," Wade told Rooster as he stepped into the stall and started brushing the horse's red hair.

"I brought you one."

Wade turned to see Nora, smiling and holding up a jacket.

"You're awesome." He grinned.

She stepped into the stall and they maneuvered the coat on him. His casted arm was left under the jacket, the empty sleeve dangled at his side which made them both smile.

"Did they tell everyone?" Wade asked.

"Jack and Reilly just got here, so they are now."

"I'm sorry Nora."

"I know…but you're a lot braver than I am, I don't know that I could have run after Bart in the dark, let alone crawl with a broken arm."

Wade didn't answer. He didn't care if he ever talked about it again.

"You done talking about it?"

He nodded.

"OK."

Nora remained quiet and brushed Dollar while he brushed Rooster.

"They sure look better." Wade commented.

"All but Arcturus," she sighed. "He's losing weight."

"That's what Uncle Grayson said. He was going to talk to Nikki about it."

"She changed his supplement plan and we're going to take him in once a week to the clinic for a checkup."

Nora stepped out of the stall and returned with a bale of straw, dragging it into the stall.

Wade smiled, she understood he needed to be with his horse…it could be the last night.

They both took a seat on the bale with Nora slipping an arm around his good one then leaned her head on his shoulder. They sat quietly watching Rooster eat.

Reilly appeared at the stall door then disappeared. He returned with two more bales and placed them next to theirs. He took a seat without saying anything. Sadie and Grace appeared next and sat with them.

No one spoke; they just watched the red horses eat.

Wade leaned his head on Nora's which was still on his shoulder. Reilly was on the other side of her. Sadie was cuddled into Wade's other side, with Grace next to her.

One person was missing…he felt his heart aching for her to be there. It wasn't right that they could be spending the last couple of hours with the horse and she wasn't there.

Then…she was. She appeared at the door, smiling at the five of them. Her blue eyes sparkled with pride and love. When she stepped through the door, she was carrying blankets.

Sadie and Grace scooted over so Aunt Dru could sit next to him. They spread out the blankets over the top of all of them.

After a few minutes, she broke the silence.

"Well, it sounds like Jordan is going to only work part time in her job."

"She said she was only going to work Tuesday, Wednesday, and Thursday," Nora added.

"How come?" Wade asked.

"Seems like we have a bunch of horses and 5 kids that are going to be doing rodeos and horse shows," Aunt Dru answered.

"Is she nuts?" Grace laughed...the laugh that made everyone else laugh.

"I think she loves all of you and wants to spend more time with you. Helping you all fulfill your rodeo and horse show dreams will do that. She'll be scheduling your shows, making sure you're in the right clubs, and driving you to them…like your manager. It's going to be quite a challenge for her."

"She's a brave woman." Reilly chuckled.

Dollar turned in the stall and looked at the group on the straw bales and stared.

"I think he's confused," Wade smiled.

"Just imagine how you would feel, if you woke up with him in your bedroom." Sadie giggled.

"I'd love that!" Wade laughed.

"How would you get him upstairs?" Nora asked, her eyes shining in amusement.

"Not so much that, as cleaning up after him…and having to haul it down the stairs." Grace laughed.

"I'd just throw it out the window." Wade grinned up at the amused eyes of his aunt.

"The guest room is underneath," she smiled at him. "I think the urine soaking through the floor might become an issue."

"I'd have done it over the summer." Sadie sighed. "Especially the first night, if they hadn't been so dirty."

"I can't believe how dirty we ALL were when we got home," Aunt Dru chuckled.

"Dad hosed off all my clothes outside before he threw them in the washer," Reilly grinned.

"Uncle Scott had to take all the trucks in twice to get the seats cleaned." Grace added with a laugh.

"We had to wash the horses twice to get all the mud off them." Sadie reminded them.

"They loved the baths." Wade nodded.

"They still do." Nora sighed with a smile.

"They love...the love you kids have given them." Aunt Dru said softly.

"You too." Wade whispered.

She nodded and kissed the top of his head.

"I wish it was still summer so we could spend the night out here." Sadie said.

"Me too." Wade nodded.

"I wish we could all go tomorrow." Nora whispered.

"But we can't." Reilly stood, walked to Rooster and lay is hands on his back.

Sadie stood and joined him...then Grace and Nora.

Tears sprung to Wade's eyes as his aunt helped him stand, unzipped his coat so his casted arm was free.

Wade walked to Rooster's front shoulders and laid his hands on the horse. Aunt Dru stood next to him and did the same.

Just as they had when Angel died, they each touched the horse and gave him their love.

***

"Can Reilly spend the night?" Wade asked Jack as they walked into the kitchen.

"Sure," Jack nodded. "of course."

Wade tried to smile, but he just didn't feel it. Besides having to leave Rooster's stall, he had to walk in to the hugs and comments from the parents about his broken arm. He just nodded but didn't say anything when they mentioned it.

"It's ten o'clock now, so you all should be getting to bed," Aunt Leah told the kids as they walked in.

The girls headed up the stairs. They all turned back and looked at him.

"Good luck," Sadie said sadly. Wade nodded.

"Come on, I'll go up with you," Jack told him.

Wade followed Reilly up the stairs, Jack walked behind Wade; an arm on his back to support his climb up the steps.

After helping him change from his jeans to his sweat pants, Jack helped him crawl into Matt's big bed and place the pillow under his cast.

Jack looked over at Reilly, who was already tucked into Wade's bed, then back to Wade.

"I wish Reilly could go with you tomorrow," Jack told him.

"Me too," The boys said in unison.

"But it wouldn't be fair to the other kids…and you'll have your parents there."

"Uncle Grayson and Aunt Dru, too." Wade nodded; then frowned. "Can you check on her before you leave?"

Jack looked at him in surprise.

"She's holding in how upset she is," Wade informed him. "She's got 'her poker face on', as dad puts it."

"I promise, I will," Jack smiled reassuringly. "But let's get you guys to sleep so your birthday gets here."

Wade chuckled; "I forgot tomorrow was my birthday."

"The big double digit!" Reilly grinned.

"Ever wonder why the double digit one is so special?" Jack asked with a smile.

"Because you're closer to being a teenager," Reilly answered.

"Because I'm closer to being able to ride with the men on cattle roundups," Wade answered truthfully. "How old do I have to be?"

Jack shrugged. "I think Matt started when he was seventeen. He was a strong enough rider and had a good horse."

"Dollar will be a good horse but I need to grow more," Wade sighed.

"You'll start growing pretty soon," Jack assured him. "You'll end up going through a couple spurts."

"A spurt?" Wade looked at him in confusion. "That's a weird word."

"Like when I grew 4 inches one summer," Reilly nodded. "Then I grew three more the next year."

"You had two spurts?" Wade chuckled at the word. "I think I might need three or four to catch up."

"Well, hopefully you get some of Scott's height." Reilly smiled.

"Just another reason to hit the double digits," Jack smiled. "So you can start your growing spurts soon."

Wade nodded. He was the shortest kid in his class. Why did his mom have to be only five feet tall?

"OK, you boys get to sleep," Jack said and headed for the door.

Wade lay in the dark looking at the ceiling...thinking of his dad.

"Thank you, Reilly."

"For what?"

"Your first big brother advise."

"I'm glad it worked...but Wade?"

"Yeah?"

"You can always trust me. Don't hold things in like that anymore."

"I won't...if Mom and Dad don't hate me after that...I can't imagine they would hate me for anything else."

"Except murdering someone," Reilly chuckled.

"Yeah...'cept that."

Wade started to drift off to sleep...

"You'll call me, right?" Reilly said as he yawned.

"As soon as I know."

CHAPTER THIRTEEN

"*This is no way to spend your tenth birthday,*" Wade thought as he moved his fingers around the coil of the lariat. It was his choice to have the surgery on his birthday and had said yes because he didn't want Rooster to hurt anymore, but now he just wished it was over.

He was in the back seat of the truck again, sitting between his parents. He was relieved that they were getting along now. Uncle Grayson was driving and Aunt Dru stared silently out the side window. Her Tagger Enterprises cap pulled low over her eyes.

All the girls were crying when they said goodbye to Rooster. They didn't know whether the horse would come home again. Wade walked to Dollar and talked to him while the girls said goodbye. All the horses were standing at the fence wondering where Rooster was going and why they weren't going too. Libby was running and bucking, unhappy they took one of her horses.

They pulled into the university a little early so Wade took Rooster for a walk before they went into the big building. He led Rooster over to the large oval arena and leaned into his big red horse. "We went to the rodeo a couple weeks ago," he told the horse. "I sat and watched all the cowboys on their horses and dreamed of us chasing the cow down the arena and roping it in world record time. We'd win rodeo after rodeo and everyone would know us."

Wade ran his hand down the nose of the horse and rubbed under the horse's round jaw. Rooster leaned into him…he seemed to know something was wrong. "I don't want you to be in pain anymore Rooster," Wade tried to hold back the tears but it wasn't working; one escaped. He rubbed his cheek on the horses shoulder to wipe it off. "I'm supposed to be an adult while we're here, but I just feel like crying like a baby," he sniffed. "Why do you think your nose gets runny when you cry?" He asked the horse. The horse answered by nudging his hands for a treat.

"I know you're hungry," he ran his hand down the length of Rooster's neck. They weren't allowed to give him his morning hay since he was having surgery.

Wade looked underneath the horse's neck and saw there were people in white coats with his parents, Aunt Dru, and Uncle Grayson. To his surprise, Nikki and Matt were standing there too. They had driven over from their university which was only a half hour away.

"Look at that Rooster… they are worried about you too." He sighed.

"Wade?" He heard his mom call out.

"I guess it's time, boy," he turned the horse and started walking back to the adults.

Wade's heart began to hurt again. Each step became harder to take and he started slowing down. It could be his last walk with the horse and he wanted it to last longer. He stopped and Rooster came to a stop next to him, with the horse's nose bumping the cast.

Not ready to let the horse go, Wade turned his back on the building and the people waiting. He looked up at the horse; his throat was tight and his voice trembled when he spoke. His big brown eyes were even with the horse's eyes and he could see his reflection. "I know, if you don't come back out, that you will be in heaven and won't be hurting anymore." Rooster rubbed his head against his chest.

Wade took a deep breath and slowly let it out. "I had a dream the other night…well, it turned into a nightmare, but in the dream I was riding you at the ranch and we were running as fast as we could. We were so happy," he wrapped his good arm around the horse's neck and took a deep breath. He wanted to remember the smell of him. He looked up into the horse's big brown eye. "No matter what happens, Rooster, I will always ride you in my dreams," A tear slowly rolled down his cheek.

"Wade," It was his mom again. He stepped away from the horse and, without turning, handed her the rope. He wanted to remember Rooster like this, not walking into the strange building. As the horse walked by, he reached out and ran his hand down the length of him. His fingers fell away from the horse's hip…the last touch. His fingers instantly felt cold so he balled them into a fist.

Rooster's hoof beats moved away from him, each step, each sound, beating into Wade's heart. "I'll ride you in my dreams…." he whispered…the hoof beats slowly faded away.

"Do you want to go in with him?" It was Aunt Dru, her voice was low and shaky.

Wade shook his head and stared at the ground. She came up beside him and stood quietly next to him.

"Remember when we first found him?" Wade asked.

"Yes," her voice was a whisper.

Wade looked over and saw her hand stretched out for his. Aunt Dru was there from the beginning and every day since. He took her hand and squeezed tightly…she understood how special Rooster was.

They walked, hand-in-hand, into the large brick building and sat next to the door where the lady told them the doctor would come out when the procedure was over.

They waited and waited.

For two hours, Wade sat and stared at the door. The lariat lay coiled in his lap. He gently ran his fingers over the ridges of the rope.

When the handle on the door began to twist, he sat up straight. Uncle Grayson and Aunt Dru were sitting next to him, pretending to read magazines, but they had been watching too and sat up. His mom and dad, sitting across from them, quickly glanced over at Wade, then to the door.

It seemed like forever before the door actually opened.

"Come on," Wade whispered. He had promised to act like an adult if they brought him. He didn't think running over to the door, pulling it open, and yelling at the doctor would be what they considered acting like an adult. He took another deep breath and let it out. He gripped the lariat tightly.

Finally the door opened and the doctor came out. He nodded at them then turned back to say something to someone in the room. There was no indication whether the surgery was bad or good.

"Come on," Wade repeated; his eyes not moving from the doctor. His heart was beating so hard he thought everyone could hear it.

Finally the doctor walked over and sat in a chair across from them. Just as the veterinarian opened his mouth to speak, Wade lifted his good hand in the air; like parents did when they wanted to quiet down the kids.

The doctor stopped and looked at him in surprise. Wade didn't notice what the other adults did.

"I'm sorry if I'm rude," trying hard to sound like an adult. Without letting the doctor respond, he continued. "I don't understand all the long words that you say, and they kind of scare me," he admitted and took a deep nervous breath; his body was tingling in dread. "I just want to know if Rooster is alive."

The doctor turned his chair so he was directly facing Wade, giving him his full attention and looked him straight in the eyes. "Yes."

Wade fought hard to keep from crying and yelling. "Is he in pain?"

"Right now he is coming out from anesthesia," He paused, realizing he had used a long scary word. "He is waking up and his legs have pain killers in them."

"I had those for my arm," Wade told him. "Will he hurt when the pain killers go away?"

"He will for a couple days, but then it will slowly go away."

Wade's eyes opened wider. "You mean he won't be in pain anymore like he was before the surgery?"

The doctor shook his head. "No, we fixed him so his joints wouldn't hurt anymore."

Wade felt his body shiver in relief.

As Wade started to ask his next question, the doctor held up his hand. "His joints won't be in pain anymore, but that doesn't fix the knees and hocks completely."

"He will still walk weird?"

"Yes," The doctor glanced up at the adults. "But the joints won't be able to take the stress of heavy weight on him or hard work."

"Doctor?" Wade asked getting his attention back. "Will I be able to sit on him until I grow up?"

The veterinarian nodded, "But he can't be ridden strenuously."

Wade cocked his head to the side. "I don't know what that word means."

The doctor nodded again, "It means that you won't be able to do things like ride him up and down mountains or run in an arena. He will only be able to walk and maybe trot with a little weight on his back."

"So, while I'm a kid, I can ride him at a walk around the pasture?"

"Yes, there shouldn't be a problem with that," the vet smiled.

Wade lifted his lariat to his lap, "I can sit on him and practice my roping?"

The doctor grinned, understanding what Wade meant, "Yes."

Wade let out a long breath and felt the stress leave with it. "When can I see him?"

"In about 15 to 20 minutes."

Wade moved the lariat over to his casted arm and stretched his hand out to the doctor like his dad had taught him. The doctor took it and they shook hands.

"Thank you," Wade smiled. "I need to go outside for a few minutes so you can say all the long scary words to the adults now." Without looking at anyone, he turned quickly and walked through the large open lobby, his boot heals hitting the ground hard and echoing throughout the room.

Once through the front doors, his pace quickened as he walked towards the truck and horse trailer. Moving behind the trailer he sat on the wheel well. He didn't want to be an adult anymore, he wanted to scream and yell like a kid.

He took a couple deep breaths to keep the tears away and started banging the rope against his legs to take his mind off the tears. Each time the rope hit his legs, his smile got bigger. Rooster wouldn't be in pain anymore. He would be fine. They would be training buddies and Dollar could be his competition horse. The three of them would be a perfect team. He jumped off the trailer and jumped in the air a couple times.

"Yes, yes, yes!" He yelled.

"Wade?" His dad's voice was on the other side of the truck.

Wade ran around the back of the horse trailer; his dad was jogging up to the trailer. Wade ran, grinning all the way and jumped in his dad's arms and they wrapped their arms around each other. Wade hugged his dad as tightly as the cast would allow.

His dad leaned back and grinned down. "He's OK," he whispered in relief. "And you came up with a great plan for him."

Wade beamed back, the happiness soaring through his body and out in his excited voice. "Can we go see him now? And I need to call Reilly."

CHAPTER FOURTEEN

Wade's eyes flickered open and he stared at the ceiling. "*It's my birthday party today.*" He sang quietly. He looked over at the window and could tell it was early. Matt was snoring on the other bed which made Wade grin. Since Wade was in Matt's bed, his cousin was laying in the smaller bed; Matt's feet dangled off the end. He came home for my birthday…just like he promised!

He lay quietly thinking of the afternoon with Rooster the day before. His parents let him stay with Rooster for hours so he could be there for the horse, like the horse was there for him. The school attendants had given him a small birthday cake since it was his actual birthday. It was in the shape of a red horse! When it was time to go, his dad had to literally carry him away from Rooster.

Wade was listening to the quiet house trying to decide if anyone was up yet. Matt had opened the window to let the cool air in, so Wade could hear cars and trucks drive by on the road. There was no sound from the house, but he heard a truck slowing down by their gate. It had to be a truck…it was too loud for a car and was definitely a diesel truck!.

He slid out of bed, stopped to make sure there was no dizziness then quickly ran to the window. It was a truck and horse trailer…and it wasn't just any truck and horse trailer! It was Jessup from the ranch!

"*Jessup came for my birthday*!" Wade yelled in his head. The cast over his hand and arm kept him from being able to pull on jeans. With his pajamas on, he pulled on his socks and grabbed his lariat. He snuck out of the room quietly so he didn't wake Matt.

He positioned his lariat over his shoulder then took off running down the long hallway and halfway to the steps, he jumped into a slide and slid on the wood floors to the top of the steps. The side banister stopped him. He giggled quietly to himself.

"Wade," he heard his dad behind him. Busted! His parents hated it when he did that.

Wade turned to see his dad standing at his bedroom door. It was slightly open and he was whispering something to his mom. He closed the door, then…took off running down the hallway, halfway to the steps he jumped into a slide and slid to the top of the steps and next to Wade. They grinned at each other.

Wade started laughing and had to cover his mouth with his free hand to keep from waking everyone up.

He turned his back to Wade. "Hop on."

Wade giggled again and awkwardly climbed onto his dad's back. They both laughed quietly as his dad carried him down the steps, setting him down on the bottom step to help slide on Wade's boots. "We have to wait for your mom."

Wade stood at the base of the steps and waited for her, "Come on," he whispered.

Jessup's truck went by the side window; Wade turned to look out the back kitchen window in time to see it stop by the barn. He started hopping in excitement and looked back up the stairs in time to see his mom suddenly appearing at the top; she had come to a SLIDING stop, her dark hair flying over her face.

She looked down and grinned. With a finger to her lips she trotted down the steps. "Don't tell your father," she whispered and gave him a big hug. "Happy birthday, son."

Wade was laughing as they walked into the kitchen. His dad was already waiting for them with the back door open so Wade ran out the door without waiting for them, and ran to Jessup's truck. The older cowboy was just coming around the backside of the trailer as Wade reached him.

"Jessup!" Wade said excitedly. "You came for my birthday!"

"That I did, boy," Jessup smiled back at him. "You look much better than the last time I saw you."

A horse whinnied from inside the trailer. It started a round of whinnies from inside the barn and the pasture. Cora's colt, Libby and Kit had come running and were standing impatiently at the gate…waiting to see who came to visit.

"You brought a horse?" Wade looked up at him in confusion. "We have fourteen horses here!" Wade reminded him as his parents walked up next to them.

"Yeah, you got a herd here, but this isn't just any horse." Jessup smiled as he opened the gate to the trailer. The door swung towards Wade, and blocked his view as Jessup crawled in the trailer.

As he stepped around the trailer gate, Wade's eyes opened wide and he took a step back. It was Monty. His pulse quickened and his heart hurt. His hand went to his chest again.

A hand rested on his shoulder, "Are you OK?" asked his dad.

Wade nodded and silently watched the big grey horse step gracefully out of the trailer. The three horses in the pasture started whinnying and dancing. Monty just stood quietly and watched them; his head high and alert.

When Wade took a step towards the horse, Monty's head turned to look at him; his big gentle eyes taking in the whole scene. Wade didn't hesitate, he walked right up to the horse and ran his hand down the grey nose. He cupped the round jaw in his hand and messaged the underside of his jaw. The horse leaned his head into Wade, letting him know he liked it. "How could I have been scared of you?" Wade whispered to him.

He turned to look at the horse's chest. There were scrapes and scratches across the chest, but two large cuts stood out where the horse had rammed the fence. Wade softly ran his fingertips over the stitches where Jessup had sewn them closed.

His dad's hand stroked the horse's neck. "He'll be just fine Wade."

Wade looked up at his dad, his big brown eyes shining, "He saved me."

"Yes, he did." His mom joined them in petting and thanking the horse that saved their son.

"Well," Jessup interrupted. "Let's get him tied up."

Jessup tied the horse to the side of the trailer.

"You want to ride him?" His dad asked.

"What?" Wade said in shock, "You said he was too strong for me."

"He is, but there aren't any cows here...you can walk him around the small corral."

"Yes!" Wade grinned. What a way to start his birthday party day!

Wade stepped to the horses head and talked to Monty while they saddled him. He told him about Rooster.

"Ok," his dad said and Wade positioned himself next to the horse. Monty was too tall for him to get on without standing on something. Plus he couldn't pull himself up with a cast on his arm.

As his dad lifted him into the saddle, Wade saw something on the leather skirt of the saddle just in front of his left knee. He leaned over and looked at the imprint. "What's that?"

"Back in the 1800's they used silver dollars for payment," Jessup told him. "That there… is a dollar coin."

Wade grinned. "A dollar?" he laughed. "You put a dollar coin on your saddle?"

"Well, not really." Wade's dad said. "Look at the saddle, Buddy."

Wade looked at the saddle again. It was a brand new roping saddle and way too small for Jessup. He turned to his parents.

"Happy Birthday!" They grinned in unison.

"Wow!" Wade smiled then looked over at Jessup. "Dollar?" Then he realized what it was. "You put Dollar on my saddle!" He said excitedly.

"Look at the other side," Jessup said with a twinkle in his eye.

Wade turned…just in front of his right knee was a rooster. "Rooster!" Wade yelled. "I have Dollar and Rooster on my saddle!"

***

It was just after lunch and Wade was waiting in the middle of the lawn where his mom told him to stand. Reilly, Grace, Sadie, and Nora were standing around him. Matt, Nikki, and Aunt Dru were standing to his left in front of Aunt Dru's truck…the door was open. A covered wheelbarrow was placed in front of them.

Jack, Uncle Grayson and Aunt Leah were standing behind Wade…another covered wheelbarrow was placed in front of them. To his right stood his dad and mom; they were next to the open gate to the pasture. The horses had been moved to the North pasture. A covered wheelbarrow was in front of his parents too.

Wade looked at each of them, wondering what they were doing. He looked around for Cora and Jessup; they were standing on the porch of the house. They had a covered box in front of them.

"Now what?" Wade asked his aunt. She reached in the truck and turned on the radio, LOUD. The music boomed across the yard. It was his favorite song, Toby Keith singing 'I Should Have Been a Cowboy'.

Wade started laughing, his toe started tapping, and his hips started swinging to the music. All the kids had started dancing and so did the parents. Everyone was singing the song at the top of their lungs.

He turned to look at Cora just in time to see something red flying toward his head. He didn't have time to move and it hit him in the forehead. Water splashed all over and was accompanied by roaring laughter all around the him.

He looked at Cora in shock. She had taken the cover off the box and was grabbing another water balloon.

Screams and laughter broke out as all the parents were throwing water balloons at the kids. The kids screamed in delight and ran for the wheelbarrows. Aunt Dru was the closest, so Wade ran for her. She handed him a balloon and he turned to throw but was hit in the chest with a blue balloon, water drenching him. He looked over and saw the culprit was Sadie. She laughed and grabbed another balloon.

Wade threw his balloon at Nikki and hit her in the back of the head. She squealed and turned to see who hit her. He looked up and saw dozens of colorful water balloons flying through the air. Wade laughed and watched Reilly hit Grace; Uncle Grayson hit Matt; Nora hit her dad; Jack hit Jessup; Aunt Leah hit Aunt Dru and it continued. He was picking up another balloon and getting ready to throw it when he heard Nora yell.

"No, Dad, No!" She was laughing and screaming. Their dad had picked her up and was carrying her to the horse's large round water trough. She kicked and hollered in fun as he dropped her in the trough. She fell with a splash, standing up quickly. Her hair was drenched and clinging to her head and shoulders. Their dad roared in laughter until he was hit in the back of the head with a stream of water from the hose, held by his wife. Wade's mom was drenched from water balloons and had run for the hose when the water balloons ran out. Wade didn't think he could laugh any harder than he was already laughing.

His mom held the hose on his dad until he charged her and picked her up. The hose went flying as he turned and started walking back to the water trough that Nora was quickly crawling out of.

"Oh, no you don't!" His mom yelled. She circled her arms around his neck and held on tightly. Wade watched as his dad kissed her and was about to turn away when he saw her arms relax and she was quickly tossed in the air and down into the tank. Water splashed everywhere.

Wade was laughing so hard he couldn't stand anymore. He fell to the ground. "Well, maybe Dad isn't so boring after all."

Check online at **www.thetaggerherd.com**
for the release date of Book Three

THE TAGGER HERD SERIES:

NIKKI TAGGER

Nikki sat back in her chair, staring at the monitor and watched silently as Jack proceeded to have the woman move the horse around the arena. The horse and rider seemed to be moving well together as the woman followed Jack's instructions. Nikki was beginning to get nervous that Jack had changed his mind, when he had them stop in the middle of the pen and he approached her. They stood quietly talking for almost five minutes; Nikki was watching the clock on the video feed. Jack was stroking the horse's neck as he was talking.

He said something that made the woman nod but Nikki couldn't see the woman well enough to see her facial reaction. Nikki sighed; they needed to get audio feed on these things too!

The rest of the appointment went without any stopping of the horse and rider. No more chats. Soon the woman slid down from the horse and stood quietly. There was no movement towards Jack, like the day before, so he wasn't being chased around the horse by her. There was no 111 call. Nikki leaned both elbows on the desk as she stared intently at the woman. From the camera angle she couldn't really tell any features about her.

At the end of the appointment, Jack reached out to shake the woman's hand. "Interesting," Nikki thought. The woman shook his hand with her right hand and brought the left hand up to touch his arm. That was an obvious gesture of flirtation. Jack didn't flinch.

"Oh, heck," Nikki was shocked. What had she started here?

Just as the woman turned to leave, the office door opened and Nikki's mom stepped inside.

"It's chilly out there," she smiled and slid out of her coat.

"But hot in the pen," Nikki sighed. "Could you hear them? Did he get any information?"

She shook her head. "I was too far away to hear the conversation in the middle."

To Nikki, that confirmed that her mother was watching as closely as she was.

A car started and Nikki turned to watch Elena Pelten drive out of the parking lot.

The door opened and Jack stepped into the office.

"Well?" They asked in unison.

He shook his head and grinned at Nikki. "As soon as I shook her hand, all I could hear was you yelling

'Don't touch her!'"

His face tinted red as the two women laughed.

"Did you find anything out?" Nikki asked him.

He slid out of his coat and sat in the chair across from her. "She's originally from Pendleton. She was just hired at the Red Lion Hotel as a sales manager. Looking for something to do, she saw The Stables ad in the flyer at the hotel. She thought riding lessons would be fun."

"Jack," Nikki asked patiently. "Is she or isn't she, THE Elena Pelten?"

"Well," he shrugged, "I know that Pelten is her maiden name."

Nikki's rolled her eyes. "I hadn't thought about it being her married name."

"Anything else?" her mom asked.

"Not really," he shook his head.

Nikki sighed in disappointment. She really thought they would have the answer today. "So, now what do we do?"

Jack shrugged, "I'll ask her more tomorrow."

Nikki sat up straight in her chair and looked at him hopefully. "She's coming back for another appointment?"

"No," Jack grinned. "I asked her out on a date."

"YOU WHAT?" Both women gasped.

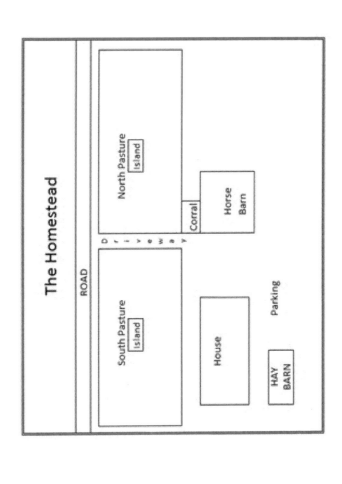

The Homestead

ROAD

North Pasture
Island

South Pasture
Island

Driveway

Corral

Horse
Barn

House

Parking

HAY
BARN

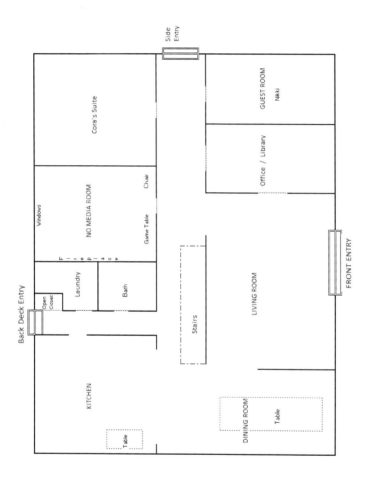

The Homestead Downstairs

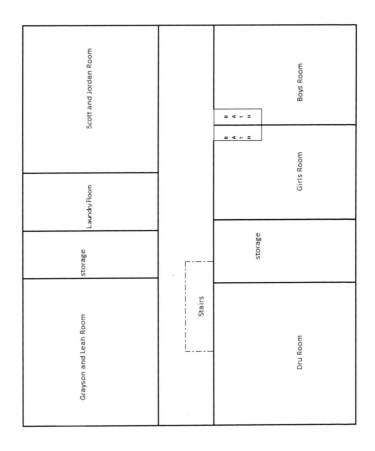

The Homestead Upstairs

The Tagger Family

Drucilla
Nikki
Matt

Grayson
Leah
Grace
Sadie

Scott
Jordan
Nora
Wade

Jessup: Tagger Ranch

Jack Morgan: The Stables
Reilly

Cora Smith: The Homestead

ABOUT THE AUTHOR

Raised with Shetlands and ponies, I purchased my first "big" horse at the age of 21…that horse (Nan) was also 21 and pregnant with Jetta. Jetta gave birth to Libby when she was 18. When Jetta passed away at 25, Libby was bred to a gorgeous palomino stallion and Miss Kit was born a year later. Three pitch black horses in a row and I now I have a bay with a tornado on her forehead! Love my girls!

Kit and Libby

My family moved to Lewiston when I was seven. I moved to Nampa and Caldwell, Idaho after high school graduation then to Alaska when I was 22. I moved back to Lewiston when I was 25 and have lived here ever since.

If you love the outdoors, this valley is a beautiful place to live. I enjoy it with my family, two horses and two beautiful Labradors; Moose and Tater.

Made in the USA
Charleston, SC
01 October 2015